The first Jake kne[...] next day was whe[...] been lying dozing and wondering if he really had to get up yet as he ached from all the peculiar exercise he had taken the previous evening. Someone outside the house was making the strangest noise. It was a mixture of crying, screaming and shouting but it seemed to be controlled and at first Jake was not sure if it was a song or a disaster. As soon as he crawled out of the house, he knew that it was not a song.

One of the young boys they had left with the cattle was standing at the entrance to the *nkang* and howling as though he was mad. His left arm had blood dripping down it and hung limply at his side. It looked broken. His face and body were smeared with mud and he was scratched all over. Jake's first thought was that he had been mauled by a lion and he made his way to Saguta, who was standing with some of his friends, to find out what was going on.

Other *Jake* books by Robin Hanbury-Tenison

JAKE'S SAFARI

by

ROBIN HANBURY-TENISON

RED FOX

For Harry

A Red Fox Book

Published by Random House Children's Books
20 Vauxhall Bridge Road, London SW1V 2SA

A division of Random House UK Ltd
London Melbourne Sydney Auckland
Johannesburg and agencies throughout the world

Typeset in Great Britain by SX Composing DTP, Rayleigh, Essex
Printed and bound in Great Britain by
Cox & Wyman Ltd., Reading Berkshire

Papers used by Random House UK Limited are natural, recyclable
products made from wood grown in sustainable forest. The
manufacturing processes conform to the environmental regulations
of the country of origin.

RANDOM HOUSE UK Limited Reg No. 954009

ISBN 0 09 925626 6

1
The Letter

'Mum! Philip! There's a letter from Kenya!' shouted Jake as he ran towards the house. He always made a point of meeting Gary, the postman, on the road if he saw him coming, taking the post and so saving him the trouble of turning into the yard. It also meant that Jake could have a quick look at the letters to see if there were any from the friends he had made on his adventures in South America and India.

'It must be from Aunt Meg,' he panted, as he ran into the kitchen and thrust the envelope at his mother. 'I hope she's coming to stay. She's great.'

'What better than me?' his mum joked. 'I know she spoiled you last time she was over!'

'Well' said Jake laughing, 'She's very different from you and we do get on really well. It's hard to believe you're cousins.' Then he gave his mother a big hug and winked at his stepfather Philip to show he didn't mean it.

'Let's see what she's got to say, shall we, before

this gets nasty,' Jake's mum laughed and she opened the letter carefully with a kitchen knife. 'You must keep all those nice stamps.'

Having no brothers and sisters of her own, his mother had spent a lot of her childhood with an aunt and uncle, whose daughter Meg had been like a sister to her. She was very fond of her cousin but they saw little of each other now, as Meg, who was a skilled nurse, worked in Africa for an international medical charity.

Jake tried to peer over his mother's shoulder as she started to read but she pushed him away.

'No,' she explained, 'I'm not going to let you see until I know what she's up to. After all, she might be telling me she's getting married at long last.'

'Okay, then read it aloud. That way you can leave out anything you don't want me to know about!'

'Don't be cheeky' said his mother, trying to sound stern, but smiling at the same time. 'Here goes. She starts . . .

Dear All,

I do wish I could see you as I miss you all horribly, especially that gorgeous nephew of mine. He's getting to be so good looking, judging from the photographs you sent me. In a few years he's going to be a real heart-throb.'

Here Jake went pink, kicked the old mangle rather harder than he meant to and stubbed his toe.

'The trouble is, I'm being kept incredibly busy here at

the moment. There's an epidemic of something rather nasty going about and we're desperately short-handed at the dispensary. It's quite safe once you're inoculated (and I have been – don't worry!) but it's a hell of a job tracking everyone down. And then lots of them have to be talked into having the injection. Meanwhile all the ones who have been done already are queuing up for a second go. I daren't leave it to Abdul, as he's more easily conned than I am.

'The thing is, I'm entitled to a free return flight home and I don't see myself using it. What do you think about . . .' Here his mother stopped reading aloud and, frowning, went on reading the letter to herself.

'What's she suggesting, Mum?' demanded Jake. 'Is she going to send Abdul over instead? He sounds like a great laugh. She told me about him last time she was over. He's got tattoos all over his chest!'

'No. She's got another idea, and I'm not sure I like it,' his mother said thoughtfully. 'I've made quite a lot of plans already for the summer holidays.'

'You mean she wants you to go out and see her. Oh you should! You'd have a great time. Don't worry about me. I'll be fine. I could go and stay with Keith on the farm.'

'No. That's not what she's suggesting either. I'd better read you what she says, but don't get excited.'

'. . . What do you think about Jake coming to stay? It's quite safe here. He can have all the necessary inoculations before he comes. I won't be able to spend all the time with him, but there are lots of friends he can stay with, and after his many adventures he's proved that he's well able to look after himself.

'Do think about it. I would love to see him and it would be such a shame to waste my free ticket. I'm not planning to ask anyone else – I'm far too busy to invite any of those numerous boyfriends you imagine I have. Anyway, I could really do with some help so you could think of it as a working holiday for him as well as being fun for me.

'Lots of love to everyone and please let me know as soon as possible what you decide. Meg.'

Jake and his mother were silent for quite a long time after she had finished reading the letter. Philip quietly left them alone, murmuring, 'This is for you two to sort out.'

Mother and son just looked at each other until, at last, she gave him a big grin and said with a little shrug, 'Oh well. I know when I'm beaten. I never could win an argument with Meg and when I have the two of you ranged against me I don't stand a chance. Only do, please, be careful. You seem to have a talent for getting in and out of trouble.'

'Don't worry, Mum.' Jake could hardly hide his excitement but knew it was best to seem relaxed at the prospect of going to Africa. 'I'll be fine. Meg's good fun and I'll enjoy helping out in the hospital. Maybe I'll decide to become a doctor!'

The summer holidays began in only three weeks, which just gave them time to book the flight to Nairobi and get Jake through his course of injections against all the things he might catch in East Africa. He also had time to spend a weekend in London with his father.

Jake's parents were divorced, his mother having remarried to Philip and moved with Jake to an old farmhouse in the country. Jake's dad's work involved lots of travel and they had been on some exciting journeys together. So he was disappointed that this summer they were not going to be able to do anything as father and son.

They always had fun together, even when it was only for a day or two in London staying in his father's flat. The hurly burly of city life was a dramatic contrast from the peace of life in the countryside and they managed to pack in a lot of entertainment. Another of the perks of Peter Travis' job was that he always seemed to be able to get hold of tickets for anything that was on, whether it was a musical or a Test Match.

When, at last, the summer term was over and the day of his departure arrived, both his parents came to the airport to see him off. It always felt a bit odd to Jake to see them together, as they had separated when he was quite young, but they got on well and never fought over him. Now his mother said, 'We've bought you a present which is from both of us for a change. You're going to see lots of wildlife in Africa with any luck and we thought the most useful thing would be a good pair of binoculars. We didn't bother to wrap them so you can carry them round your neck and use them to look at the ground as you fly south.' He thanked them both and gave them each a big hug. They were miniature field glasses but very powerful and with an infra-red coating on the lenses to protect his eyes from the sun.

'You *have* got your Swiss Army knife with you, haven't you?' asked his father.

'Yes, Dad. It's packed because otherwise it would set off the alarm and they'd take it off me in case I hijack the plane,' Jake replied deadpan.

His mother and father both groaned. 'Very funny Jake, considering all the things that usually happen to you on your travels! Anyway,' his father continued, 'you don't really need much else, do you?'

'Most of my luggage is presents for Aunt Meg. With all the food you're sending, you seem to think there's nothing to eat in Africa. Don't worry, I'll be fine. And I promise to take care.' Out of habit, Jake crossed his fingers behind his back as he said this. He was really looking forward to another good adventure. It had been a year since the last one.

As the plane flew south, Jake looked down on the endless barren wastes of the Sahara desert, where ancient dried up river beds meandered through the sand-dunes, and he wondered if he would have a chance to get out into the real country. He hoped he would, as the prospect of spending a whole month helping Meg in the hospital was not one that appealed to him as much as he had pretended. But he had a feeling that things would not turn out that way.

2
Africa

Nairobi airport was bedlam. Jake stood still holding firmly to his suitcase as the multi-racial crowd milled around him. A couple of large black men in khaki tried to persuade him to get into a taxi. He told them firmly but politely that he was waiting for someone and they left him alone. He was just beginning to wonder what he would do if Aunt Meg failed to turn up, when she arrived in a great flurry and swept him up into her arms.

'Jambo Jake! And how's my favourite nephew?' she asked breathlessly as she hugged him.

'I'm your only "nephew" and where were you anyway?' Jake gasped as he wriggled away. Meg gave a great laugh. 'You haven't changed a bit, my darling. Just better looking than ever.' That shut Jake up and he followed her meekly through the crowd, lugging his heavy suitcase.

Meg was wearing khaki safari clothes and she exuded confidence. Her face was sunburnt and weatherbeaten and she walked fast, so that he had trouble keeping up. She seemed to know everyone at the airport and several times she stopped for a moment to have a quick word or crack a joke with an official as they walked past. This gave Jake time to catch up. There were lots of four wheel drive vehicles lined up outside, their drivers loading them up and, again, Meg had something to say to most of them. Jake knew that she had been in Africa for several years and it began to dawn on him that she was not only well liked but something of a star. 'That Meg,' he overheard one of the tour operators say as he passed, 'I don't know how she does it, but it's good to know she's out there if anything goes wrong.'

'It's a long drive we have ahead of us,' she told him as they climbed into her Land Rover, 'so we're going to stop at a Game Lodge on the way. That'll give you a chance to see some wildlife and get a feel for Africa. It's run by friends of mine and it's very luxurious. Enjoy it while you can. It's a lot different from what you're in for up north.'

They were soon out in the country where, once the houses were left behind, the road was bordered by lush small holdings, trees and tall crops of maize and banana. Beyond were dry, barren hills but every inch of land near the road seemed to be cultivated. And there were people everywhere: laughing faces crowded around the vehicle whenever they had to stop, offering trinkets for sale or just reaching out to shake hands. When they pulled up to buy some fruit at a roadside stall, Jake thought they were going to be mobbed, but Meg said a few sharp words in Swahili which made the crowd roar with laughter and back off.

'What did you say?' asked Jake.

'I just told them that I planned to kidnap one of them to take on Safari!'

'Will you teach me some Swahili, please? It obviously helps when people know you're not a tourist.'

'Sure does. Sure will,' replied Meg cheerfully, as she waded through the crowd and started haggling over the price of some bananas and oranges. 'Meanwhile eat this. It's a long time till supper,' and she threw him an orange.

While waiting for Meg at the airport, Jake had unpacked his Swiss Army knife and now had it in his pocket. Taking it out, he began to peel the orange and eat it. Feeling his sleeve being tugged, he looked down to see a very small boy with big round eyes staring up at him. Once he had Jake's attention, he sat down on the ground and held up his left foot. Stuck in the sole was a nasty thorn and the boy made it clear with gestures that he wanted Jake to pull it out for him. He took the tweezers out of their slot in the body of the knife, put it down on the ground and carefully extracted the thorn from the boy's foot, holding it up to show him once the job was done.

Suddenly, the boy leapt to his feet, grabbed the knife off the ground and ran off.

'Oy!' shouted Jake at the top of his voice. 'Stop thief!' and out of the crowd stepped Meg just as the small boy was dashing past. She stuck a foot out, tripped him up so that he sprawled in the sand beside the road and dropped the red penknife, which lay in full view. For a moment no one moved. Then Meg bent down and picked it up, the boy scuttled away and everyone burst out laughing.

'Looks like you fell for the oldest trick in the book, you twit!' she said to Jake. 'You're going to have to do better than that out here or you'll lose your head next,' and she gave him back the knife. Jake, who was still holding the tweezers, put them back in their slot and looked suitably ashamed of himself.

'Don't worry,' Meg grinned at him. 'You'll learn. Meanwhile put your knife on this lanyard and tie it to your belt. Then even *you* can't lose it.'

She undid a length of strong cord from around her waist. It had a clip on one end, a noose on the other and was long enough to reach from Jake's belt to the breast pocket of his

11

bush shirt. When this was buttoned down the knife was safe and easy to get at.

Jake was very tired after his long journey and found himself dozing off and on for much of the rest of the trip. This was pretty amazing considering he was bumping about in the front of the Land Rover as they drove along a road full of potholes. When the going became much worse, he sat up and rubbed his eyes to find they were driving on a rough track towards a river with thick forest on both banks. The open countryside away from the river had huge, fat trees dotted over it. They looked a bit like ancient English parkland oaks, only with much bigger trunks than any Jake had ever seen.

'What are they?' he asked, and Meg told him they were baobabs, one of the most remarkable and valuable tropical trees.

'Your mother must have read *The Little Prince* to you when you were small. Don't you remember the trees that were always threatening to take over his tiny planet? Actually, they are wonderful plants. The fruit are edible, that bulbous trunk is full of water and there are all sorts of things like cloth, rope and even paper that can be made from the bark. We call them "upside down trees". There's a legend that the devil pulled up the first baobab, pushed its branches underground and left its roots in the air. I love

12

them. So do monkeys. Look! There are some in that one.'

Jake could see several creatures hiding in the branches and they drove closer to have a better look. Using his binoculars he had a really good view and could see that they were beautifully coloured monkeys with a greenish tinge to their fur.

'Describe them to me,' said Meg. 'I can't see them very well from here.'

'Well,' said Jake, holding the glasses steady and focusing them carefully, 'they're monkeys and they have long tails with a curve at the end. They've got black faces with a sort of white ruff around which makes them look rather posh. Only they're making silly faces at me, raising their eyebrows and grinning, which spoils the effect a bit.'

'What about their rear ends?' asked Meg.

'Mmm, yes,' Jake hesitated, 'their bottoms are pretty colourful,' he finished, laughing.

'I knew it,' exclaimed Meg. 'They're my favourites, vervets. They're real show-offs. Just wait and watch.'

Sure enough, the monkeys began to gather close to the Land Rover, making faces and leaping up and down, swinging from side to side, twittering and screaming. One old male strutted about presenting his backside, an impressive and colourful sight which made Jake laugh, and a couple of the younger males started throwing nuts and twigs down at the vehicle.

'Time to go, I think,' said Meg. 'I'm glad you saw that.'

They drove on and soon came to the game lodge belonging to Meg's friends. After the dry countryside they had been driving through and the scruffy villages of the tin shacks they had seen, it seemed very luxurious. There were green lawns with sprinklers spraying great jets of water, which made rainbows of the evening sun. The buildings were thatched and had wide over-hanging eaves, giving lots of shade to sit under and sip drinks. And there was a beautiful swim-ming pool which, as he was hot and sweaty after the long drive, Jake begged to be allowed to dive into.

'Better wait until you've met Dick and Jenny,' said Meg. 'They may have something even better planned for you.' The Wilsons came out to greet them and showed them to their rooms, which were simple but very comfortable. Jake rummaged for his swimming trunks as soon as he put his bag down and asked, 'Is it OK if I go for a swim?'

'Of course,' replied Dick Wilson, 'but if you want to go on a game drive you'll have to be quick. We plan to leave in about fifteen minutes. I was afraid you were going to miss it.'

'We stopped to look at some of those vulgar

monkeys on the way and they got a bit excited,' explained Meg.

'Typical, if you were encouraging them,' laughed Jenny. 'You're incorrigible Meg. You spend too much time in the bush. What you need is a good holiday. You bring her down here Jake and we'll all have some fun.'

Jake realized that the Wilsons were very good friends of Meg's and he relaxed. He had been feeling a little nervous about being on his own in Africa with someone he called 'Aunt', but didn't really know as well as he might. But now he could see that she was completely at home and well able to cope, whatever happened. He raced to the pool and dived into deliciously cool water. Three fast lengths and he was out again and drying himself.

Grabbing his field glasses and his knife, he ran towards a strange vehicle full of people who were waving at him. It was a big Jeep with a roof which lifted on struts so that some of the passengers could stand up and look out.

'Jump in young fella,' shouted an American voice, and a big, friendly bald man leant down to give Jake a hand. 'You stand there up in the front. I hear you've only just arrived in Africa and so you should have the best view. Don't you agree everyone?'

There were welcoming murmurs of agreement from the rest of the party and Jake was introduced to the two couples whose tour this was.

'It's very kind of you to let me come along,' he said politely, realizing these were paying customers and that he was getting a free ride.

'Not at all young man. It's good to have you with us. Just hold tight and I think you're going to enjoy the next hour.'

3
The Game Driver

The driver was an African ranger called Joseph. To begin with Jake had some difficulty understanding what he was saying; then he got the hang of the accent and listened intently as Joseph revealed his vast knowledge of everything they passed.

'This is acacia woodland we are going through. If you look closely you can see some sunbirds feeding there in that bush.' At first Jake could see nothing. Then a flash of scarlet and yellow drew his eye to a small bright green bird with brilliant markings in a band across its chest.

'That is the Beautiful Sunbird,' said Joseph.

'I can see it's beautiful,' said one of the Americans, 'but what's its name?'

'That *is* its name,' explained Joseph. 'There are all sorts of sunbirds here. I can see a Malachite over there – do you see, it's all green? And that's a Collared Sunbird there with the yellow belly and a violet band on its breast.

They are all beautiful, but the first one we saw is actually called Beautiful.'

Although he was using the glasses, Jake could only just make out the details Joseph was describing, and yet he seemed able to tell what sort the birds were just by glancing at them.

'How do you know which they are so quickly?' Jake asked him. 'I find it all very confusing.'

'You will get used to it quickly. I have lived here all my life and I know all the creatures very well. It's easy for me.'

They drove on towards the river and then, as they came round a clump of thorns, Joseph slowly allowed the vehicle to stop. Everyone was silent and clearly looking at something, but for a moment Jake could see nothing except the scrubby bushes. Then he realized that just beside them was the tallest animal he had ever seen. It was standing so still and was so well camouflaged that he had thought it was a tree and not looked twice. Now he saw that it was a huge giraffe towering over them so that he had to crane his head backwards to look up at its head. It was gazing curiously down at him from big soft eyes, around which Jake could clearly see long black eyelashes. Above the eyes were short horns with black tufts of hair at the ends and there was a neat mane running down its long long neck. But it was the sheer size of the animal which had silenced everyone and for a while it seemed they were all holding their breath.

Then someone moved to lift a camera and without any apparent effort the vast creature very gently turned away from them and seemed to glide across the ground in a series of gentle bounds.

'That was the Reticulated Giraffe. They are quite common; but you were lucky to see one so close. Usually they keep further away from the Jeep. I think this one must have been asleep.'

'Do they sleep standing up?' asked Jake.

'Yes, they can if they want to, but sometimes they lie down for a bit, too,' replied Joseph. 'Now let's see if the hippos are expecting us.'

They drove on to a low bluff overlooking the river and looked down on a big lagoon full of weeds, waterlilies, rushes and strange grey shapes, which Jake assumed were rounded stones showing above the surface. Suddenly one of the shapes rose up with a great splash and they all recoiled as a colossal mouth opened and a loud roar like a cow bellowing came out of it. The inside was bright pink and seemed to have huge curved teeth on both sides.

As they watched, the pool came alive and the hippos started to flounder about. Some dived and disappeared completely for much longer than Jake could imagine being able to hold his own breath. Others joined in, with mouth

19

opening and roaring, which seemed to turn into a competition to see who could make the most noise. Over in the shallows some babies played, sliding in the mud and trying to climb on top of each other. Just as quickly as it had started, the activity suddenly stopped and the pool was quiet again. Anyone arriving then would have been unaware that there were any hippos there at all, just grey shapes in the mud.

'Good timing eh?' said Joseph with a grin. 'They do it just for me you know,' and he winked at Jake.

It was beginning to get dark and so they headed back towards the lodge. On the way they saw several herds of impala which ran away in a series of extraordinary high leaps.

'Why do they do that?' Jake asked Joseph.

'Probably to confuse anything chasing them and to see where they're going. It's called "pronking". I don't know why, but it describes what they are doing rather well, don't you think?'

Just as the light was going, Joseph gave a sigh and slowed the Jeep down to a crawl.

'I hoped they would be here,' he said softly. 'Can you all see them?'

Everyone had to confess that they couldn't see whatever it was he was looking at. He pointed and said, 'Look there, on that little sandy mound. Two lions.'

And then they could all see. There were two lionesses lying side by side. Their heads were up and they were looking ostentatiously in the opposite direction, as though deliberately ignoring the intruders into their domain.

'This would not be a good place to get out and stretch your legs,' said Joseph. 'They have a kill nearby and they might think you were going to take it. I think it's time we went home.'

Jake was barely able to keep awake during supper, which was full of talk about all the wonderful things the guests had seen that day. He excused himself early and went to bed. There was a mosquito net over it and a green coil under it, which had been lit and gave off a little wisp of smoke to keep insects away. But before he turned out the light he wrote everything he could remember in his diary. He had promised his mother that he would.

'This time I want to know all about what you get up to,' she had said. 'Not just the bits you choose to tell me!'

4
Lipi

Before the rest of the guests had woken up the next morning, Jake and his aunt had quietly packed and were ready to leave. They joined the Wilsons in their kitchen for some coffee and Dick said, 'If you get bored with Meg, you can always come back and stay here for a bit. I'm sure we could find something useful for you to do.'

'Oh please, Meg, can I?' pleaded Jake. 'I could drive the Jeep so Joseph could spend his whole time spotting things for the tourists.'

'No you could not!' replied Meg rather quickly. 'What's the matter, you bored with my company already? And anyway, when did you learn to drive?'

'Well, there is that,' Jake sighed. 'Don't worry, Meg, I won't abandon you just yet!'

'Glad to hear it,' Meg smiled. 'Now then, let's get this show on the road!'

'Good lad,' whispered Dick as they loaded the Land Rover. 'You take care of your aunt. She works incredibly hard and she's very tough but we do worry about her. Health is a big problem out here and she is one of the few really dedicated nurses around. As a result she just never stops working. I know she's been really looking forward to you coming out. Anyway, you're still welcome here any time, but try and get her to come too and take some time off.'

'Thanks a lot,' said Jake and he dashed off to find Joseph, who he had spotted crossing the lawn.

'I might be coming back for another visit,' he told him, 'then I could help you.'

'That would be good, Jake,' Joseph replied gravely. 'I could certainly do with an assistant,' and he shook Jake's hand.

The long drive through the heat of the day was uneventful. The countryside became more and more barren as they headed north, until at times they were driving through stretches of desert. Approaching vehicles could be spotted at a great distance by the dust clouds they put up and a couple of times they passed camels being driven along the road. The camels were led by tall, dark men who, unlike everyone else they passed on the way, did not smile and wave but stared straight ahead.

'Who are those people?' Jake asked.

'They are Somalis and they shouldn't really be here,' answered Meg. 'They are very tough people and they lead very harsh lives, always wandering with their herds of camels, as well as cattle, sheep and goats. Their country is away to the east and there is a lot of fighting going on there. There always has been and now it's worse. It makes life very difficult for them, so that sometimes they prefer to come over here and steal cattle. When they do that we call them Shifta, which means bandits. Everyone is a bit afraid of them as they have guns, which the Maasai and Samburu can't easily get, thank goodness. Otherwise, there would be a full-scale war. But I do wish the Shifta would go away. They frighten me.'

'So who does this land belong to?' asked Jake.

'We are entering the Northern Frontier District which has always been fought over. This part is occupied by the Samburu and the Maasai, who migrated here hundreds of years ago from the north. They live for their cattle, which they love, and they spend all their time looking after them. They don't grow crops and they don't wander as far as the Somalis. This is their land. The trouble is that, thanks I suppose partly to people like me bringing hospitals, the populations of all these people are growing – Kenya has one of the fastest population growths in the world – and so the competition for land is getting worse. There just isn't enough grazing to go round and so there's quite a lot of fighting.

But don't worry. We have no quarrel with anyone. They all come to the hospital to get patched up!'

They began to see groups of Maasai and Samburu from the road. Usually they were standing on one leg, guarding their cattle some distance away. They looked very colourful with bright red blankets draped over one shoulder and Jake wanted to stop and talk with them, but Meg wouldn't let him.

'We're in a hurry, I'm afraid,' she explained. 'You'll get plenty of chances to meet some of them when we get to Lipi, the village where my little hospital is. They are mostly Samburu there, though, even after all these years, I find it hard to tell the difference. In fact, there's a Samburu boy who sometimes helps me out in the dispensary. He can take you to meet his family.'

Jake's first impression of Lipi was of disappointment. It was a shabby place, just a wide street lined by dirty single storey huts, mostly made out of concrete with tin roofs, although a few were of mud and wattle and thatched. Meg's little house was not much better. It was in the hospital compound, where there were a few dried up trees, but the inside was bare, with just the minimum of furniture and some brightly coloured rugs. Jake suddenly wondered what he was going to do with himself all day.

As though reading his thoughts, his aunt said, 'I'm hoping to be able to take lots of time off so that we can go and stay with more friends like Dick and Jenny. I know a huge number of people and we can have loads of fun. But first I have to go and check up at the hospital what's been happening while I've been away. Why don't you come and meet everyone?'

'Everyone' turned out to be an elderly Italian doctor called Carlo; Abdul, Meg's assistant; and three very jolly Kenyan nurses called Eunice, Esther and Rose, who fussed over Jake and made him feel about six years old. There was a ward with half a dozen very sick people in it. Their relations were camped outside and Meg explained that most patients came to their clinic during the day with few staying for any length of time.

'Fortunately, we're not very busy at the moment and so we should be able to get away soon. Meanwhile, where's Saguta?' she asked one of the nurses, who pointed to the end bed of the ward. An old man was lying very still, while a boy of about Jake's age sat on a chair beside him reading aloud from a book in a quiet voice.

'Hello Saguta,' said Meg. 'Sorry to interrupt, but this is Jake. How is your grandfather?'

The boy stood up and Jake realized that he was quite a lot taller than him and very thin. His hair was neatly wrapped in what looked like a tea towel and his ears were pierced so that there were quite large holes through the lobes.

'Hi,' he said as he shook Jake's hand, 'I heard you were coming. You are very welcome.' Then, turning to Meg, he said in a lower voice. 'Grandfather Lacanta is much better. I am reading him a book from school about the history of our people. It is in English and I am translating as I read. He does not agree with what it says. I think it is good for him to be a little angry.'

'Well don't make him too angry,' said Meg. 'We don't want another incident!' And they grinned at each other like conspirators.

'What was that all about?' Jake asked, as they made their way back to Meg's house.

'Saguta's grandfather is a wonderful old man, but he has never been in hospital before. He hates it and we have the devil's own job controlling him. Last week he got up in the middle of the night and decided to go home. He woke everyone up crashing about, disturbed the other patients and nearly got himself shot by our night watchman. Saguta is the only person who can keep him quiet. He seems to be doing a good job at the moment and the old boy really must stay for a few more days until he is stronger; but I don't expect we'll be able to keep the old rogue much longer than that. He's nearly better anyway.'

'What was wrong with him?' Jake asked.

'Malaria. It's a big problem here. He also had a rather nasty gash on his leg. You *are* taking your pills aren't you? It's important.' Jake assured her that he was. 'It makes you terribly weak, malaria, and that's not very dignified for an elder, which is one of the reasons he's in such a bad temper. Saguta is a great lad. He's also very bright and can tell you much more than I can about his people. I've asked him to take you to meet his family some time. Meanwhile, I'm going to be busy catching up and I want you to come with me on my rounds. Then, in a few days, I hope we can take off into the bush.'

'That'll be great,' said Jake, cheering up. 'Have you got a TV?'

'That's something you're going to have to learn to do without, my boy,' laughed Meg, giving him an affectionate cuff. 'We don't even have electricity most of the time as the generator keeps breaking down. But I've got lots of books, especially ones about Africa, and you have a lot to learn, judging by your performance so far!'

Jake had seen so many new animals since arriving in Africa that he sat up late poring over Meg's book, comparing the pictures with his confused memories and wondering if he would ever sort it all out.

'You'll get the hang of things eventually,' said Meg as she looked in to say goodnight. 'Everyone does in the end.'

28

5
Nursing

When Meg had said that she wanted Jake to help her, she had been serious. 'There's no place for freeloaders around here,' she told him in the morning. 'I need every single pair of hands and it's time you learnt what medicine is all about. Just warn me if you're going to be sick.'

'I won't be sick,' protested Jake. But he nearly was, almost as soon as they started examining the first patient.

Meg's surgery was a bare room with a shiny metal table, a sink, a locked cabinet of medicines and a sterilizing box full of surgical instruments. When they arrived after breakfast they found Abdul fussing about, scrubbing the surfaces and chasing out the flies. He was a jolly little man in a clean white uniform who spoke English very fast and very loudly. As they crossed the hospital compound they could hear him shouting, 'Keep out! Keep out! I am the only one allowed in here.' A row of people dressed in a mixture of colourful robes, rags and suits sat on benches outside. One young man was lying on a stretcher and he was brought in first. A dirty cloth, stained with blood, was tied around his shoulder and arm. When Abdul and another man had eased him on to the table, Meg carefully undid the cloth and they all peered at what was underneath. The first thing that struck Jake was the smell. The wound was very messy and it was clearly infected.

'What did this?' asked Meg.

'Simba!' the men who had carried the stretcher replied eagerly. 'Lion!' They seemed really pleased about it, as though the fact that the patient had been mauled by a lion somehow made his wounds honourable.

'How long ago?' Meg asked them, grimly.

The answer took a long time, but it seemed that the young man, who was from the Meru, a settled people who grew crops, had been pounced on by a lion while walking back from his small farm three days before. It had taken that long to get him to a road and then to per-suade a truck to give him a lift to the hospital.

'I hope I can save his arm,' muttered Meg. 'Lion bites are horribly poisonous. I will have to work fast,' and she began to clean the wound. Jake watched for a time, feeling helpless and sickened by the sight of the badly mangled flesh. But Meg, catching sight of his expression, immediately sent him on a series of errands: to fetch more dressings and to warn them at the hospital to prepare a bed, so that he was soon too busy to feel sick.

After the Meru had been stitched up, a process Jake decided not to watch, given a hefty dose of antibiotics and sent off to the ward, there were all the other patients to see. Many seemed to have nothing wrong with them and Jake was impressed by the way Meg seemed able to get to the heart of their problem in the minimum time. Some she would talk sharply to, clearly giving them a rocket for wasting her time. To others she listened carefully and then took her time preparing some medicine and explaining how it should be taken.

'How do you know which ones are having you on?' Jake asked, during one of their brief rests.

'I can pretty well tell by now, but I have to admit, sometimes its guesswork!' she replied with a smile. 'The trouble is, there simply isn't time to give everyone a fair hearing. If I did, no one would get treated at all.'

During the afternoon Jake helped Abdul around the hospital compound while Meg visited the patients in the ward. Most of the work they had to do involved clearing up the rubbish that the patients and their visitors had brought into the compound. Abdul's uniform was not now as clean as it had been in the morning, having been spattered with blood and iodine during the morning's surgery. When they found a blocked drain which had to be cleared by pushing a rod through it, Abdul took off the top of his tunic and revealed the famous tattoos which Jake had heard about through one of Meg's letters. They were impressive, being a mixture of abstract designs and colourful birds and animals, and they covered the whole of his torso. Across his back was an elephant wrestling with a large snake. The snake and the elephant's trunk were entwined and disappeared into Abdul's trousers.

'Wow, Abdul!' Jake exclaimed admiringly when he saw them. 'How did you get those?'

'I have had them for many years,' Abdul replied, clearly pleased to have them noticed. 'I had them done in Madagascar when I was a young man and worked as a sailor. It makes me very attractive to the ladies.'

'So do all the nurses fancy you, then?' Jake replied.

Abdul looked cross at this. He knew that Jake must have seen the nurses laughing at him behind his back and he answered stiffly, 'Those nurses do not understand what a responsible job I have and they do not show respect. I have had to speak about it to Meg many times.'

Later that evening, when he and Meg were having supper, Jake asked her about Abdul.

'He is a really good sort and I couldn't

possibly manage without him, but he does take himself dreadfully seriously. The girls probably know more about medicine and nursing than he does, but he likes to be in charge and so we all put up with his ways. He is also very good at all the languages we have to use here and so he always knows exactly what is going on, as well as being very useful.'

Jake learned just how useful the next day, when Meg took him and Abdul on a medical tour of some of the surrounding villages. At each one, a crowd began to gather as soon as the Land Rover drove in. They all wanted to tell Meg about their ailments and they all seemed to be speaking different languages. Abdul would jump up on the bonnet of the vehicle and harangue the crowd. Under his instructions they would form a queue of sorts and he would never let them near Meg until they had first told him what was wrong with them. This information he would then relay in a loud voice so that all present could hear. To Jake's surprise no one found this in the least embarrassing, even when some of the ailments were pretty personal.

'This man says he has a blockage and has not been able to do anything for a week. This one says he has the opposite and cannot stop going. This man has a boil on his bottom and cannot sit down.'

Then there were the peculiar ways some

described what was wrong with them. Abdul had been told by Meg never to try and interpret what they meant but simply to translate literally what they said. Jake listened amazed as he heard:

'This one has mice in his head which are eating his brains.'

'What on earth does that mean?' he asked Meg.

'That's easy,' she replied with a laugh. 'Have you ever heard a better description of a headache?'

There were people with rats in their stomachs, ants all over their bodies, wives inhabited by devils and cattle which were bewitched. One old man complained that whenever there was thunder it entered his body and made him shiver.

'It's probably malaria,' said Meg, 'but what matters is that he believes it's thunder and so I must agree with him.'

She dealt with everyone sympathetically but without wasting any time, so that a huge number had been seen and a lot of medicine handed out before they drove back to Lipi in the evening. Then it was time to check the ward patients and see if any problems had come up during the day. Dr Carlo, who was well past retirement age and should, as he kept telling everyone, really be back in Italy, spent most of his time in his office. He had a bed there and seldom went out. Meg would sometimes consult him about a difficult case, but most of the time he left everything to her.

This frantic routine went on for nearly a week. Jake found it all fascinating but he was beginning to wonder if he was ever going to have any fun. He always looked forward to seeing Saguta in the ward as they got on well and the Samburu boy was full of stories about what life was like out in the bush where his people lived. He, too, was becoming restless looking after his grandfather and he was itching to go home. The school he attended in Lipi during term time had broken up and there was nothing more to keep him there once his grandfather's wound healed. The trouble was, he was such a bad patient that it was taking longer than expected.

Then, on the evening of the sixth day, Meg came over to the old man's bed, where the two boys were talking across him. 'You've both been very good and helpful. Thank you. I think you both deserve some time off. Saguta, why don't you take Jake home tomorrow? We can look after your grandfather and Jake has certainly earned a break.'

'Will it be all right with your parents?' asked Jake, and Saguta replied, 'Just you wait. You'll see that it's *always* all right where I live!'

That night Saguta's grandfather ran away from the hospital. His absence was discovered at midnight and there was a lot of excitement as everyone looked for him, but he had disappeared into the bush.

'Oh well,' said Meg as they went back to bed, 'he's not really quite ready to go home yet, but at least you can tell Saguta that he doesn't have to come back with you tomorrow. He'll be pleased, I know.'

6
Saguta's People

Jake was not at all sure what to expect when Saguta came to fetch him in the morning, just after Meg had left for work. She had given him some Kenya shillings and told him that they would be going by bus and staying the night, though he had no idea what was going to happen. But Saguta was in a good mood, clearly excited at going home, and Jake felt ready for anything which, as it turned out, was just as well.

They were dressed the same: bush shirt, trousers and trainers, and both had small bags with a change of clothes.

'I'm going to spend the next few weeks with my people,' he explained. 'School's over until the end of the holidays and there's nothing to keep me here any more now my grandfather's run away. I expect he's back home by now. He gave them a really hard time!'

There was a crowd at the bus stop with people loading baggage on to the top and some climbing up to ride there too.

'It's much more fun up there, but Meg made me promise to make sure you sat inside as it's too dangerous she thinks,' said Saguta. 'We'd better not get into trouble too soon!'

They pushed their way into the bus and found two seats together near the back. Across the aisle from Jake was a huge woman with a basket of chickens on her lap, and in the seat behind was a man with a young goat held firmly between his legs. The noise was deafening, with everyone shouting at once and a few scuffles breaking out as people fought over seats. The heat and the smell were as strong as any Jake could remember, but everyone was laughing and joking, and he suddenly felt happy that at last he was really in Africa, not just looking at it as a tourist.

'How long's the journey?' he asked.

'Only about an hour,' replied Saguta. 'I hope you don't mind?'

'Not at all,' laughed Jake. 'This is what I came for.'

'No it isn't,' said Saguta, looking serious for a moment. 'Just wait till you get to my place.'

It was a long, bumpy ride. Everyone talked and clambered about inside the bus, and a couple of people were even sick. Dust blew in through the open windows and Jake watched the landscape. It seemed extraordinarily harsh and dry, so that he could not imagine how anyone could survive in it. Just thorn scrub, bare brown earth and spreading acacia trees, which gave a little shade. There were nearly always hills in the distance, which looked more promising. Some had green vegetation on their slopes below sheer cliffs.

'Where is everyone?' asked Jake. 'It all looks empty to me. I thought Africa was teeming with life.'

'It is,' replied Saguta, 'you just can't see it yet. There are lots of animals out there, and lots of my people, too. This our land and we keep moving about all over it. We are a nomadic people and our land belongs to all of us. No one just owns a little bit. You will see.'

At last the bus stopped and Saguta nudged Jake, who had dropped into a doze, and said, 'This is where we get out.'

No one else got off and suddenly they were alone, apparently in the middle of nowhere, with the bus just a cloud of dust disappearing into the distance. Without a word, Saguta set off at a fast pace along a faint track, and Jake followed him.

They walked for half an hour without speaking much. When Jake asked, 'Is everything all right?' since Saguta seemed preoccupied, the reply was, 'I never feel at ease in the bush when I am dressed in European clothes. I have no weapons with me and there are lions about.'

'I've got my Swiss Army knife,' said Jake as a

joke, holding it out. But Saguta's look of scorn shut him up and they strode on in silence.

Just when Jake was beginning to work up a sweat as the heat of the day gathered strength, Saguta paused, looked around him and said, 'We'd better sit here under this tree for a bit while I tell you a few things about my village and my people. We are quite close now.

'You may be shocked when we arrive. You will find it very different from what you are used to – and you will find me different, too. But pleased do not be afraid. I am your friend and I will not forget that. But my people are very proud and very traditional. It takes a little time for them to accept strangers.

'I am fourteen years old, like you, but four years ago I was circumcised and I became an *Imurran*, a warrior.'

Jake found this conversation rather embarrassing, but Saguta appeared to find nothing odd about it and carried on.

'When I am at school in Lipi I try to forget about all that and get on with learning, although it's difficult sometimes. But when I get home, I will begin to change. Fortunately none of my *laji*, that is, my clan, those who were circumcised with me, will be there. They are out looking after the cattle, which is what we do until we become elders in about ten years time, after the next *laji* of warriors is made. Until then we do

40

everything together and our first loyalty is to each other. It is a very good time for us, though very hard too. I wish I could spend all my time with the cattle, but my father says I must go to school.

'My village is called a *nkang*. There, we will sleep in my mother's house tonight, because you are with me. Normally, I would sleep with my *laji*. I think you will be okay because Meg has told me about all the places you have travelled and the adventures you have had, but just remember that we are a very proud people and we know that our way is best, even if it is not the way you do things in Europe.'

'Don't worry, Saguta,' replied Jake seriously, 'I'll do my best to fit in – but thank you for warning me.'

When, a little later, they stopped again on a slight rise and Saguta pointed saying, 'There is my *nkang*!' Jake could only see an endless vista of varied bush, through which ran a dried up river bed.

'Can't you see the smoke?' said Saguta, pointing again, and then Jake could see, beneath a faint haze, a cluster of brown huts. They looked tiny and almost invisible, blending perfectly into the landscape.

'Wow!' Jake exclaimed. 'How many people live there?'

'About forty. You'll be surprised how efficient

it all is' and he took a deep breath. 'Well, here goes. Let's meet the village!'

The settlement was surrounded by a thick thorn stockade. The minute they stepped inside, they were engulfed by barking dogs, quickly followed by a group of small, shouting children. Then a tall distinguished looking man with a blanket over one shoulder and wearing a green felt hat, came out of one of the huts, looked at them for a moment and then began to speak to Saguta in the Samburu language. After a short exchange, he came over to Jake, shook hands and Saguta said, 'This is my father. He does speak some English.'

'You are welcome,' said the tall man with a formal smile. 'Please come inside.'

Jake had to duck to enter the house through the low doorway. The roof was smooth and rounded, covered in what looked like mud but what Jake found out later was dried cow dung. There were skins hanging down the inside walls and, at first, it seemed pitch dark. Jake stumbled over something, hopped over a fire, which he suddenly saw in front of him and, finding that the ceiling was too low to stand up fully, collapsed on to a raised platform. There was a shriek of laughter from a figure Jake could just begin to see as his eyes became accustomed to the dark.

'This is my mother,' explained Saguta. 'I think

you must have trodden on her!'

'Please say I'm so sorry, but I can't see a thing.'

'Don't worry. She understands and says you are to sit down and have something to eat and drink.'

It had been a long morning and Jake was feeling thirsty, so he gladly took the gourd Saguta's mother passed him and drank deeply from it. It was cool and refreshing. 'That was delicious,' he said. 'What was it?'

'Blood, I expect,' replied Saguta. 'Let me have some.'

Jake held his breath for a moment and wondered if he was going to be sick. He knew that the Maasai and the Samburu drank blood fresh from their cows and he had realized he might have to do the same, but he had not prepared himself for the experience.

'You really should have warned me,' he said in an anxious voice, not wishing to offend Saguta but at the same time feeling he'd been put in a very difficult position.

'Would you have drunk it if I'd told you what it was?' asked Saguta grinning.

'Probably not, but that's no excuse.'

'Yes it is; because that's what you'll get lots of while you're staying here and my mother would think it very rude and strange if you refused. It's what we drink. Actually, it's about half and half blood and fresh milk. Very nourishing! Now you know how good it is we won't have a problem, will we?' Jake had to reluctantly agree that he had a point.

At first a lot of other things about the *nkang* seemed very strange to Jake and he was shocked that someone like Saguta, who seemed so western, should think of it as home. Then he began to see how clean, well organized and comfortable it really was. Although the houses were small, there were quite soft places to sit, and the ground, both inside and out was swept clean so that there was no litter or dirt. There were some big black flies which annoyed him a bit but there were few smells, except for the quite pleasant background aroma of cattle and goats. The woodsmoke bothered Jake a bit at first, as it made his eyes stream. The dogs, once they had accepted the new arrivals, kept well out of the way and the small children were well behaved. In fact, he realized, it was the behaviour of the people which made it all work so well. Everyone moved slowly and politely. It was a very peaceful place.

Saguta's mother was beautiful and serene. She smiled at Jake in the most friendly way, talked to him gently in Samburu and kept pressing food and drink on him. There was a haunch of smoked meat – goat, Saguta told him – hanging over the fire. She would slice piece after piece off with a sharp knife and pass them to

Jake. It was just like the best beef sandwiches, he thought, only without the bread. And the blood and milk tasted better and better in the darkness, rather like unsweetened milky coffee. He found himself nodding off so that when Saguta said, 'Look, why don't you have a rest while I look around? This is where we will be sleeping anyway,' he mumbled his agreement and dozed off.

7
The *Nkang*

'Come on Jake! Time for some exercise,' said Saguta as he shook Jake awake. 'The children have spotted a honeyguide and we're going to follow it.'

'What's a honeyguide?' asked Jake as he followed Saguta out of the house.

'I'll explain as we go, but now we must run to catch them up,' and they dashed together out of the stockade and hurried along a sandy path. They could hear the excited voices of the children ahead of them.

'Honeyguides are strange birds but very useful. They're a bit like your cuckoos as they lay their eggs in other birds' nests, but their special talent is finding wild bees' nests. When they do, they come and tell us by singing to us and fluttering about. Once they get our attention and we start to follow, they will lead us to the bees. The children are following one now.'

Soon they caught up with the young children, who pointed excitedly at a rather plain brown bird about the size of a thrush which was chattering loudly and hopping from bush to bush ahead of them. They all followed for a while, and then one of the children gave a shout and ran towards a larger, dead tree around which some bees could be seen. The honeyguide now stopped singing and perched quietly on a nearby branch, watching.

The nest was spotted some way up the tree in a crack, from which the bees flew in and out in a steady stream. There was some discussion among the children until Saguta, who had been standing aloof from them with Jake, gave an order.

The largest child gathered up some dead grass, which he placed around the foot of the tree and then lit it from a smouldering stick which another child had carried from the village and kept alight. Smoke curled up the tree trunk and bees poured out of the crack to fly around fast outside the smoke.

When it looked as though most of the bees had left, the boy discarded the ragged cloth he wore tied around his waist, rubbed earth on his body with some broad leaves which smelled and oozed a sticky juice, and then he began to climb the tree. As he neared the nest, bees darted into the smoke which enveloped him and some clearly got through as he yelped and slapped at himself. But he persevered, reached the nest and quickly scooped it out with a stick which he broke off a dead branch. Boy and nest hit the ground almost simultaneously, and he ran off a few yards slapping at his body.

Another boy threw more grass on the fire and fanned the smoke towards the nest, which had broken open on impact to reveal several large combs of honey. The rest rushed in and grabbed these, getting a few stings at the same time but extracting most of it before the bees started swarming all over the base of the tree.

The combs were brought to Saguta, who was treated with a good deal of respect by the children. He inspected them and pointed at one which had white larvae showing. It was taken and thrown near where the honeyguide was perched. Immediately, the bird hopped down and began to peck at the larvae and the surrounding wax.

'It is very important to do that,' explained Saguta. 'Otherwise, next time the bird will get its own back by leading us to a buffalo or a lion!'

The children poured the rest of the honey into a gourd and carried it back to the *nkang*, where they were made a fuss of by the women, who came out of their houses to greet them. Jake had not seen the other women of the village properly before, as he had gone straight into Saguta's house. Now he noticed that they were all wearing rows of beautiful coloured beads around their necks, had bangles on their wrists and ankles, and there were more beads in their hair and hanging from their ears.

'Have they dressed up specially?' he asked and Saguta laughed. 'No. My people are always beautiful. Just wait until you see the men!' Jake thought he was joking as he had never seen such colourful people. As they came out of their houses in their blue and red robes, laughing and dipping their fingers in the honey, they seemed like a flock of butterflies and he told Saguta that this was what they reminded him of.

'Funny you should say that,' was the reply. 'They say that the name for my people, Samburu, comes from the Maasai word for a butterfly – *sampurumpuri*. It sounds like a butterfly flopping along doesn't it, or so my teacher said the other day in school, but we don't call ourselves that. We call ourselves *lokop*, which means that this land is ours. But I still say wait until you've seen my *laji*!'

As the light began to fade, the old men and the women brought the sheep, goats and a few cows which had been grazing outside the stockade, in through different entrances to the boma, penned them in more small circular enclosures made from tightly packed thorns and started milking them. A delicious smell of roasting meat came from several of the cooking fires.

That night, inside their house, Saguta and his

family sat around a warm fire and told stories. Some of them he translated for Jake; at other times they just talked among themselves, while Jake wrote up his diary by the light of the fire, trying hard to remember all the things he had seen and done during the day.

'They are talking about the flies,' said Saguta. 'They noticed that you were swatting at them today when they landed on you. We do not do that as we believe that before there were any cattle there were only flies. The flies were a sign that the cattle would follow and so we put up with them. You must try and learn to do the same while you are with us. You will find life is much easier if you do not let them annoy you.

'Now they are talking about our god, Ngai,' Saguta said, some time later. 'He is everywhere: in the trees, the rocks, the rivers, the springs, the animals and in every person. We feel him everywhere, but if you want to feel him most strongly, you must go to the top of a mountain. That is where he lives.'

'Just like the Greek gods on Mount Olympus,' murmured Jake, who had been doing ancient history the term before at school.

Gradually, people slipped out of the hut or just snuggled down and went to sleep. It was wonderfully relaxed, Jake found. Everyone was absolutely free to do as he wished in his own time. Yet there was a sense that there was a right way to do everything and he was glad that he had Saguta there to guide him. He put his diary away, took off his clothes, wrapped himself in a blanket and fell asleep to the comforting sound of voices softly droning on about Samburu legends. 'Now,' he thought as he drifted off, 'I really am in the heart of Africa.'

8
A Change of Plans

Jake crawled out of the hut before dawn, still wrapped in his blanket, as it was cold outside. There was a thin mist over the ground and he sat for a while watching the sky begin to lighten. Others were beginning to stir and some of the animals in their tight pens were moving about and making soft noises. Inside the protective thorn fence of the main stockade it felt wonderfully secure, as though this was the way people had always lived.

He watched as a goat was quickly slaughtered by Saguta's father. Within minutes, the blood had been collected, the skin removed and pegged out to dry, and the meat shared out among the families.

Saguta's mother came outside carrying some gourds. She smiled sweetly at him and went over to one of the pens. She led out a tall white cow with a pale brown face and began singing softly to it. The cow stood still, contentedly chewing its cud as she leaned against its right flank and began to milk it straight into one of the gourds. Jake wondered if he should offer to help, but he had seen enough of Samburu life to learn that this would probably not be the right way to behave. As she milked three cows in turn Jake noticed that she took milk only from the right two teats and let their calves drink at the same time from their mothers' left teats.

As she passed Jake carrying the three full gourds, she passed one to him and motioned him to drink. It was simply delicious, hot and frothy, just what he needed to drive away the morning's chill.

They had to leave soon after to catch the bus to Lipi. 'Please come and stay for longer when you and Meg get back. I want you to meet my *laji*,' Saguta said, sounding as though he meant it. 'I'm sure you will have a great time with her, but this is the real life and you fit in better than I expected. Just as long as you remember that the Samburu are better at everything you'll be all right.'

'I'll bet you're not better at running than I am,' said Jake, who had won the school cross country race and reckoned he could beat Saguta. 'Race you to the bus!'

They were both pretty fit and it was a good race but they both began to realize as they neared the road that neither really wanted to win. Jake felt that it would be rude after being allowed to stay with Saguta's family, something he guessed no other foreigner had been invited to do; and Saguta because the Samburu are not very interested in winning races. There are much more important ways for them to show their superiority. And so they contrived to arrive together at the place where the bus had dropped them off the day before, both making a great show of trying, but ending up collapsing on the ground laughing.

'Do come back. I mean it!' shouted Saguta as Jake climbed into the bus and it roared off in its usual cloud of dust.

Meg was waiting when he arrived in Lipi and she drove him back to her house, looking rather grave. 'I've got bad news, I'm afraid,' she said. 'I was really looking forward to taking off with you – I certainly need a holiday – and I thought everything was set up. But I've just heard that there's an epidemic up country and there's no one else who can go. They say children have started dying and I simply have to be there, but I don't want to take you as I promised your mother I wouldn't put you in any danger. And, to be honest, it really wouldn't be much of a holiday for you, would it? The trouble is, I haven't a clue what to do with you. There just isn't time to take you down to Dick and Jenny's as I have to leave first thing in the morning and there's no else I can ask.'

'Don't worry,' replied Jake. 'Calm down. Saguta's last words to me were an invitation to go back – and I know he meant it. I really liked it there and I'll be perfectly happy with his family until you return, however long it takes. I know how to get to his village now, and I'm sure I can find my way from the bus.'

'No. That's too dangerous. I'd worry myself sick not knowing if you had got there safely. But there is another way, if you're sure you want to go there. The police found Saguta's grandfather, the old rogue, after he ran away, and he's back in the hospital now. It's really more trouble than it's worth trying to keep him any longer and so if you took him back to the village, I'd be sure you were in good hands. He'd know that if anything happened to you I'd have his guts for garters!' And for the first time since his return, Jake saw Meg smile.

So it was that twenty-four hours after leaving the Samburu *ngai*, Jake was back, walking along the faint trail towards it once again. This time, he had as his companion a very bad tempered old man, who muttered constantly under his breath as they walked quite slowly along. They stopped quite often for rests, which Jake pretended he needed as he could see that the old man was in pain but too proud to admit it. Their final stop was under the tree where Saguta had told Jake about the *nkang*.

The old man was becoming excited as he neared home. He pointed down towards where it lay hidden in the bush and made a long speech to Jake, which, of course, he couldn't understand a word of. Then suddenly he stopped and stared hard at something moving away from the village. Leaping to his feet with more energy than he had shown all the way, he began to stride off the track on a line to intercept what he had seen. Jake hurried along with him and, as they drew nearer, he could see that it was two Samburu warriors. They stopped and waited for them to approach.

9
Saguta

During his first visit to the *nkang* Jake had admired the way the women and the old men decorated their bodies with beads and red ochre. Even the children had made their bodies more beautiful with paint, rings and tufts of grass. And he had been impressed by how elegant everyone was all the time, even when doing something messy like gathering up cow dung and being all covered in flies. Their brightly coloured shawls and their leather or red and white cloth skirts were always draped stylishly and they stood tall and proud.

The figures coming towards them made all the other Samburu Jake had seen look scruffy. They seemed to glow with light and colour and to glide over the ground. They were tall and slim. Each carried two long spears and had a short sword at his waist. This stuck out of the clean red and white striped cloth which was all they wore. One's head was all bright red, delicately painted with ochre on the skin. The other had long hair hanging down his back, braided into fine strands and glistening with more ochre laid on thick. The top of his head had been shaped into a sort of visor, like the peak of a cap. A stiff strip of animal skin had braids of hair laid over it and was held together with lots of bright buttons and coloured bits of leather. Each had round pieces of shining white ivory through the lobes of his ears and strange designs were painted with great detail on their faces. Around their heads, necks and arms were rows of vivid red, white, blue and green beads. They were, Jake thought, almost too beautiful to be human, and yet they gave off an aura of confidence, strength and serenity which made the English boy suddenly feel inferior and ugly.

'Sopa!' called out the old man beside him, and the warriors grunted loftily 'Sopa' before halting a few yards away. They stood on one leg, one foot pressed against the other knee and gazed into the distance for a moment. Then, suddenly, the one with long hair let his shoulders relax and he turned towards them with a broad grin on his face and said 'Hello Jake! You didn't stay away long. Have you come back to be a Samburu?'

'Saguta?' gasped Jake. He could not believe that the heroic figure in front of him was the same person as the schoolboy in ragged shorts that he had raced to the bus the day before. 'What have you done to yourself? You look great. It must have taken ages.'

'Most of the morning. But you see my cousin and I are going to rejoin our *laji* and I must look my best. Do you want to come with us?'

'Can I?' asked Jake. He had assumed he would be living with Saguta in his *nkang* and he was not sure his aunt would have allowed him to go back if she had known he would be herding cattle. But without Saguta life would be difficult and boring. 'Are you sure your *laji* won't mind?'

'Normally they are not friendly to outsiders, but you are my friend and they will accept you. I will ask my cousin to go with my grandfather, take your bag to the *nkang* and tell my father where you are going. He will catch us up again in no time. You will need nothing from your world while you are with us, except perhaps that useful little knife. We can give you all you need to live like a Samburu. You just have to do everything I tell you!'

'That could be a problem,' retorted Jake, and the boys grinned at each other, 'but let's give it a try.'

For a time Saguta talked to his grumpy old grandfather, who would clearly have preferred to come with them. Then Saguta's cousin picked up Jake's bag disdainfully, holding it by the straps so that it bounced along the ground and they separated.

'It's a good thing I've got nothing valuable in

it,' said Jake as they watched them disappear and, with a final glance at his last link with his own familiar world, he took a deep breath and said 'OK Saguta, I'm all yours. Make me into a Samburu!'

'I could never do that; there's far too much to learn. But we can have a lot of fun trying. Now, let's go and join my world.' And he started heading steadily towards the horizon, his eyes fixed ahead and an expression on his face which was at the same time eager and tranquil.

Jake found he could easily keep up, walking beside Saguta most of the time and only dropping behind when they followed narrow trails through bush. They did not talk much, saving their breath. Once Jake asked, 'How do you know where to go?' and Saguta replied, unhelpfully, 'I just do.'

Every so often they would cross dry river beds where the sand lay smooth and soft. These were like main roads running through the countryside and sometimes they followed them for a while. The sand became very hot as the day wore on and Jake was glad of his trainers. He noticed that Saguta and his cousin, who had caught them up, were wearing sandals made of some sort of skin.

'These are made from cow leather,' he explained. 'In the old days we used giraffe hide, which was the best, but hunting is now forbidden and most of my people now use cow leather, while some like the rubber from old car tyres.'

At about mid-day, they came to a place where someone had been digging into a river bed and had reached water. The two warriors immediately lay down and drank some, scooping it up in their hands, and so Jake did the same. It was clear and free of mud, having filtered through the sand. It tasted wonderful and was quite cool. Jake splashed water over himself, but the Samburu only drank as to wash would spoil their beautiful decorations. But even so, some time was spent before they set off touching up the paintwork with little wooden spatulas produced from behind their ears.

They saw little wildlife as they strode along through the heat of the day. Whenever something moved in the bush as they were passing, or if they heard a sound, Saguta and his companion would immediately turn with one of their spears held at the ready. Jake felt hopelessly inadequate when this happened and he would wait, conscious of being useless, until they continued on their way. When he told his companion what he was feeling, Saguta answered mysteriously, 'We're going to have to do something about that, aren't we?'

There was no time to worry much about what lay ahead as Jake was too preoccupied making sure that he did not stumble or make a noise as they walked. He felt it a matter of honour to show that he was as good at moving silently across country as the Samburu and, by and large, he was quite pleased with his performance.

'We're nearly there,' said Saguta. 'I can smell the cows.' Jake sniffed, but there was such a mixture of strange scents in the air: flowering scrub, tree bark, earth and his own sweat, that he could detect nothing new. A few moments later they came round a bush and found themselves surrounded by cows. They stopped while the cattle, their heads all lifted together, stood motionless and gazed at them. Saguta looked carefully around, his eyes stopping briefly to take in each cow. Jake could tell that he was looking at them with great affection.

A voice broke the sudden silence and a Samburu warrior, dressed and decorated similarly to Saguta, strode into the clearing and looked at them in surprise. Saguta spoke to him and immediately, with a huge grin, he came across and greeted his fellow *laji*. 'Sopa Murata!' they called out to each other. Completely ignoring Jake, they started chatting eagerly, only breaking off when three more young Samburu joined them. Saguta had a lot to say, and it was not for some time that Jake, who had sat down on a log, realized they were talking about him.

Now they all looked at him, jerking up their

chins and with far from friendly expressions on their faces. He was beginning to wonder whether coming had been such a good idea after all, when Saguta called him over, saying 'Don't worry. They're just not used to outsiders dropping in.'

10
Jake Joins the *Laji*

As they drove the cattle slowly back to their camp, the young warriors took it in turns to walk with Jake and get to know him. To his surprise, most of them spoke some English and they quizzed him about where he came from and what he was doing there. When he told them he was Meg's nephew, and Saguta had confirmed this and said a whole lot more in Samburu, they all had to shake his hand. They were full of stories of how she had helped their families through various gruesome injuries and illnesses. Jake was glad she was so popular and secretly vowed to try and keep up his family's reputation.

The camp was simply an enclosure of thorns into which the cattle were driven at night. They found several young boys there who were spending time with their older relations, learning what life would be like once they, too, were circumcised. Three more groups returned with their cattle and there was a lot of bustle as some of the cows were milked while others had some blood taken from them. This was done by tying a leather thong tight around a cow's neck so that the main artery stood out. An arrow with a sharp rounded head was then fired from a tiny bow at very close range. As the arrow bounced off the cow's neck, it was followed by a gush of bright red blood, which was deftly caught in a gourd. The small wound was then staunched by having a finger pressed to it and the litre or so of blood was stirred with a stick. This, Saguta explained, was to remove the fat. The stick was thrown to some dogs which fell on it, growling and fighting over it.

In Jake's honour some dried meat was boiled up in a pot with various green plants and herbs and, after drinking their blood and milk, everyone feasted on this.

'Normally we live on blood and milk only,' Saguta told Jake. 'You'll get use to it, but tonight we're making an exception.' Jake was beginning to find the whole situation so strange that he no longer cared what happened next. His companions were now friendly towards him and the atmosphere, as it grew rapidly dark, was like that at the beginning of a party.

'If you are going to learn to be a Samburu, you are going to have to start looking more like one,' Saguta told him, laughing. There was a lot of discussion and some running about between

65

the warriors' scattered possessions, and then they gathered around him expectantly.

'They have collected all you need from spare things they have brought with them and now they are going to kit you out.' Saguta could barely control himself as he saw Jake's startled expression.

'You will be much more comfortable dressing as we do and you will not look so different.'

'I don't want to offend you,' Jake said, embarrassed. He had noticed that none of the warriors wore anything under the loose pieces of cloth which they either draped over their shoulders or tied around their waists, 'but I would like to keep my trousers and I don't think my feet are up to your sort of sandals yet.'

'OK, you can keep your shorts and your trainers on if you like, but you must take that shirt off and put this over yourself. It's called a *shuka*.' And Saguta passed him a large piece of bright red cloth. 'Apart from anything else, it's what you'll be sleeping in.'

Jake took the cloth, removed his shirt and draped the material over his shoulders. It felt soft and warm. He was already glad of it as the evening cooled down. Someone had lit a fire and now they all gathered round it to warm themselves, but they were not finished with Jake.

Several objects were laid out on the ground in

front of him and he realized they were the necessary items of equipment for a Samburu.

'This,' said Saguta picking up a short sword, 'is called *lalema*. You will carry it with you all the time and sleep with it beside you.'

Jake took it and looked at it carefully. It was sheathed in a leather scabbard and there was another very small knife stuck under the leather strap. The sword itself had a double blade and both were as sharp as razors.

'What do I need this for?' Jake asked.

'For fighting!' was the alarming answer.

Next, he was given a magnificent spear. It was almost two metres long, but light and easy to carry. One end was simply a pointed piece of metal but the other had a sharp blade covered with protective strips of leather. With the spear came a long stick which, it was explained, could be used as a weapon or for driving the cattle.

Finally a *rungu* was tossed to him. 'That,' said Saguta with a laugh, 'even little children need, but it can also be a very useful weapon.' It was a short stick made out of hard wood and with a big lump at the end. Every Samburu male carries one from earliest youth as his main weapon. It can be thrown end over end with extraordinary accuracy and can also be very effective at close range.

'Now,' said Saguta, alternating between English and Samburu for the benefit of the others sitting around the fire, 'you can pretend to be like us. We are like birds that fly and wheel around the sky. We are swifter and cleverer than all the animals and our cattle are the finest. To be a man you will have to kill a lion with your spear. When you do so you must cut off its right ear and put it on the end of your spear. But I think you will never be a Samburu,' he finished.

Jake felt that they were half laughing at him, but also that there was no cruelty in their laughter. They just felt hugely superior to him and found it funny that anyone should even try to be as great as they clearly thought themselves. He privately decided that he was not going to let them prove him weaker than them, although he knew he had a great deal to learn.

For a long time they all sat around the fire, which was kept up by the small boys, who were sent off at regular intervals to fetch more firewood. One after another they sang and Saguta faithfully translated everything for Jake. He was clearly very proud of the songs, which he explained were made up by his friends and were special to that *laji*. Jake found them rather boring as they all seemed to be about the same things: their cattle and how brave they were when fighting. He found himself getting drowsy and Saguta noticed. Making a space for him to lie down, he fetched a soft animal skin onto

which Jake rolled. Before he knew it he was
sound asleep, lulled by the singing and
exhausted by all the walking and the new
experiences.

11
The Ceremony

Jake awoke to find that dawn was breaking. Already, while he was still asleep, the *Imurran* had quietly milked the cattle and he felt ashamed that he had slept through the noise they must have made moving the animals around. He had slept well on the ground, wrapped in his red cloak. He stretched and stood up, suddenly realizing that, for the first time in his life, he did not have to get dressed: he was already wearing what he would be wearing all day. He tied on his sword, picked up his spears and strolled over to where Saguta was milking a cow. Passing him a gourd of hot, frothy milk his friend said with a smile 'So what are you missing from your world?'

'I could do with a toothbrush,' replied Jake, who always felt guilty if he forgot to brush his teeth.

'No problem,' replied Saguta. 'Here, use this,' and he tossed over a short piece of wood.

'What is it?' asked Jake.

'It's called *nkiki* and it is our toothbrush. Haven't you noticed that everyone has one and chews it all the time?'

Come to think of it, thought Jake, he had noticed that many of the people he had seen since he had arrived at the airport had been chewing on a twig, but it had not occurred to him to wonder why.

'That's why we've all got such good teeth,' laughed Saguta, 'and it tastes a lot better than toothpaste.'

To Jake's surprise he found, when he tried chewing the end of the stick, that it did indeed have a rather nice taste, fresh and sharp; and, after he had practised for a while, his teeth felt as clean as he could remember them after a really good brushing.

'What's up today?' he asked.

'Well, normally we would drive our cattle to a new pasture, watch over them and, perhaps, gather some plants and seeds for food or for medicine. But my whole *laji* has decided to return to the *nkang* as I brought them news of a big ceremony being held there tonight.'

'You mean we have to walk all the way back when we've just got here?' Jake exclaimed.

'It's not that far and you will enjoy the ceremony. We wouldn't miss it for the world.'

The *Imurran* gathered up their spears and were ready to leave before the sun had begun to give out any heat. They summoned the half dozen small boys and spoke to them sharply and loudly, telling them that they were in charge of the cattle and not to let them out of their sight. The children were grinning excitedly at the prospect of being on their own but they stood up tall and looked important as their older relations slipped away in twos and threes. Normally, Saguta explained to Jake, they would never dream of leaving their cattle with nothing but boys to protect them and, in fact, another of their *laji*, who had injured his foot and could not walk, would be staying with them. However, the ceremony was one they all wanted to attend and they would only be away for the one night.

Once again, Jake followed Saguta and they did not speak much.

'What's this ceremony about?' he asked once as they were resting for a moment in some shade.

'It's about marriage,' replied Saguta, 'and it's very important for us; but I don't expect any of the girls will even look at you. After all, we are so much more beautiful!'

If Saguta had said that a couple of days ago, Jake felt he might have been insulted by such a remark. But now, looking at his friend, Jake found it hard not to agree.

'We'll see about that,' he said, with all the confidence he could muster and he decided privately to keep out of things as much as he could that evening.

When they arrived at the *nkang* during the afternoon, they found that lots of young people of both sexes were already there. The boys and girls kept well apart, talking in groups or helping each other with final touches to their spectacular body decorations. All the young men were as elaborately painted as Saguta and the girls, too, were covered in beads, jewellery and red ochre paint.

'Normally, we are not allowed to mix with the girls. We do our things and they do theirs. But today is special and we will be mixing.'

Towards evening everyone went outside the *nkang* to some flat ground, which was bare and free of weeds. The *Imurran* gathered at one end and the girls formed a group at the other. They were all excited and chattering together as the tension mounted. Suddenly one of the young men broke into a chant and immediately the others joined in. They all began to beat out a rhythm, stamping the ground with their feet and tapping their *rungus* against their spears. They were looking across at the girls, grinning and preening themselves. It was quite clear to Jake that each one was making out that he was the most beautiful of all. He found it embarrassing at first and kept away from the group of his new friends, standing half out of sight beside a tree.

With a sudden rush, one of the warriors danced forward, leaving his companions and skipping towards the girls. To Jake's astonishment, he suddenly leapt high in the air, turned and danced back to his group just as another set out to do the same.

Time after time they followed each other out into the space between them and the girls, jumped straight up with arms hanging down and looking directly in front and then returned. All the time the noise was getting louder and louder until the whole plain seemed to be vibrating with it. Jake found himself taken over by the rhythm, so that he was tapping his feet and his spears. He even chanted, although he had no idea what he should be saying, and he found, after a time, that he had joined the group of dancers.

Now the dance changed. The groups of warriors and of girls came closer together and there were a series of individual songs. Saguta was so much a part of what was going on that there was little time for him to explain or translate for Jake. He gathered, however, that once again the songs were all about their cattle and their bravery. Some of the girls sang and chanted too. There seemed to be a lot of teasing going on.

The atmosphere became more and more frantic and the dances more and more energetic. One or two of the boys fell down in a fit and had to be carried away, but no one paid any attention: they just went on dancing. Now they were leaping again, a strange stiff-legged leap which projected them quite high in the air to land again and bounce back, rather like a pogo stick. Jake thought it looked easy, until he found himself being pushed forward and having to do it himself. It was not at all easy to jump high from a standing start, but he did notice that the girls seemed to surge forward with particular interest whenever it was his turn.

'Be careful!' Saguta whispered in his ear. 'If one of the girls really likes you, you will have to marry her. They have never danced with a white boy like you before and I think they are interested.'

The dancing went on far into the night and only ended when everyone fell exhausted to the ground, many sleeping where they lay, out in the open. Long before that, Jake had crept into Saguta's mother's house and made himself comfortable by the fire.

The first Jake knew that something was wrong next day was when he heard the wailing. He had been lying dozing and wondering if he really had to get up yet as he ached from all the peculiar exercise he had taken the previous evening. Someone outside the house was making the strangest noise. It was a mixture of crying, screaming and shouting but it seemed to be controlled and at first Jake was not sure if it was a song or a disaster. As soon as he crawled out of the house, he knew that it was not a song.

One of the young boys they had left with the cattle was standing at the entrance to the *nkang* and howling as though he was mad. His left arm had blood dripping down it and hung limply at his side. It looked broken. His face and body were smeared with mud and he was scratched all over. Jake's first thought was that he had been mauled by a lion and he made his way to Saguta, who was standing with some of his friends, to find out what was going on.

'Bad news, I'm afraid,' his friend told him. 'We should not have left those young boys alone. Somali robbers came in the night and attacked the camp. They fired guns, terrified the boys and stole the cattle. They will be driving them away towards the border now. What is even more terrible, they shot the warrior with the cattle, as he was unable to run away.'

'What are we going to do?' asked Jake. 'Send for the police?'

'It would do no good,' replied Saguta sadly. 'They are not from here and they do not know our cattle like we do. No. We must go ourselves as we have lost our honour by letting them be stolen. Tell me. Do you have a gun?'

Jake was so surprised by the question that he

did not reply for a moment. Seeing this, Saguta explained.

'You see, they will have guns and without them we will find it more difficult. But our spears will win. I know it.'

At that moment a strange hooting sound came from outside the *nkang*. One of the old men was blowing through a long curly trumpet made from a horn. 'That is our kudu horn,' said Saguta. 'It is only blown at important ceremonies and on special occasions like this. We had better get there quickly.'

The elders were gathered under a big tree a little way from the *nkang*. Saguta told Jake this was the meeting tree where all important matters were resolved. The elders did not look at all pleased. Apart from the loss of the cows themselves, they were ashamed at losing something so valuable as cattle to people who would not know how to look after them or understand them. For the Samburu their cattle are everything and nothing could replace the part they play in so many people's lives.

First of all, the boy who had brought the message from the camp was shouted at and abused until he was close to tears.

'I think that's unfair,' protested Jake. 'The little ones clearly never stood a chance; and anyway, I think he was pretty brave to come back all this way in the dark on his own.'

Saguta explained what had happened as the story was extracted from the boy. The evening before, just as it was getting dark, the boys had been about to close the entrance to the thorn enclosure around the cattle. A group of about eight Somalis had charged in, firing guns and screaming at the tops of their voices. The little boys had been terrified and had lain down on the ground and hidden as the bullets crashed around them. Jake remembered what it had felt like to be shot at when he had been in South America* and he could understand how scared they must have been and he could not blame them. The *Imurran* had stood up bravely and he had been shot. He himself had had his arm broken by a club as he tried to duck past one of the invaders.

The survivors had hidden in the bush and watched as the cattle were let out of their enclosures and driven off. They had decided that he would run back to the *nkang* with the news while the others followed the invaders to see where they went.

Then it was the turn of the *Imurran* and Jake went with them in front of the head man. Although he could not understand a word, the rocket they were given was impressive to Jake. He could feel his companions quail under what

*Jake's Escape

78

felt like physical blows as the elders continued to lambaste them.

Then all at once it was over and everyone moved to a cleared area back in the village. Here the elders had prepared a circle of cow dung, into which all the young men crowded. Soon they were chanting again. Jake was amazed at how much fitter he was than he had been at the start.

'What's going on now?' asked Jake.

'We are praying to Ngai, our God, to protect us; and the elders are blessing us.'

'Does that mean we are going?' asked Jake. 'If so, then I'm coming too.'

'I don't think that's a very good idea,' replied Saguta looking gloomy.

'Well I'm not staying here on my own, I can tell you and, as Meg's away there is nowhere else for me to go. I'm coming.'

'It is for the elders to decide,' replied Saguta. 'They are gathering again. We must go and ask them.'

All the boys stood silently while the elders debated. It seemed to Jake that they took a long time discussing everything, as he was impatient to be off, but Saguta explained in a whisper that nothing was ever decided without the elders' approval. He noticed that the younger men were very polite and deferential to the elders and never argued with them.

The question as to who was to go in pursuit was the main issue. It was resolved that all Saguta's *laji*, the warriors responsible for leaving the cattle and coming to the ceremony, should go.

'Please tell them that, as I was there too, I am also responsible and wish to go,' said Jake.

A heated exchange followed Saguta's translation.

'They are worried that they will be blamed if anything should happen to you. Also, that you will not be able to keep up.'

Jake looked at his friend. 'Only you can persuade them that I am as fit and as strong as you. Even if it is not absolutely true, please tell them I am. I must come with you. Say also that I will leave a letter explaining that I insisted on going.'

Eventually, thanks to Saguta's powers of persuasion, it was agreed that Jake could go. In no time, he had scribbled a note to Meg. It read:

Dear Meg,

I know you will be angry at my going with the others, but you would do the same. They tried to persuade me not to, but I insisted. I will be all right – and we won't tell my parents!'

Then they were off. Jake wanted to take his rucksack, but Saguta said 'There is nothing in it you will need and it will slow you down. We Samburu can find everything in the bush. It will be hard but I will show you how to live properly.'

And so, dressed as a Samburu and carrying nothing but his spears, Jake set off behind Saguta. As he looked back for a last glimpse of the village, he thought how much he had changed in the week since he had arrived in Africa. When he had first seen it, the *nkang* had looked to him like nothing – a scruffy collection of poor hovels. Now it felt like home and he knew that if he had chosen to stay, he would have been perfectly comfortable there. Instead, he had chosen to trust himself to a group of boys barely his own age and to go with them on a dangerous mission into a dangerous desert. But he felt no fear. He already knew enough about his companions to be convinced that he could not have been in better hands.

12
The Chase

They jogged along in silence. The pace was much faster than when he had been walking behind Saguta before, but Jake found that the excitement of the chase stopped him feeling tired. At first his bones ached. He developed a stitch a couple of times and had to stop, bent over double, until it went away. Then he began to get into his stride and found that he had no more trouble keeping up.

They passed the camp, looked at the traces of the fight and saw the body of the boy who had been killed. Some elders had come with them to carry the corpse back to the village for burial. Jake looked at the bundle wrapped in its cloaks and thought how tragic it was that he should have died so young. And, with a growing feeling of trepidation, he began to realize just how serious the situation really was.

'What will happen to him?' he asked Saguta.

'There will be much mourning and the elders will perform special ceremonies for several days under the meeting tree. This way we will all be blessed and our people will be united.'

'Will he then be buried?'

'No. He will be carried out into the bush and the wild animals will take care of him. That way he is always with us. Only very old and important men are buried.'

From then on they were following the trail of their cattle and they spread out over a wide line.

'The Somalis are clever,' explained Saguta. 'They know that we know more or less where they will be heading – the Somali stronghold – after which we cannot follow them and our cattle will be lost for ever. But there are several routes they could take and if we lose their trail, it will be hard to pick it up again. They cannot go as fast as us, since they are driving cattle, but they do have a full day's start.'

They ran on until well after dark on the first night before coming together and lighting a fire. There was not much to eat, just some strips of dried meat and a few handfuls of meal called *posho* which they had brought with them, as well as a sip or two of milk and blood from the gourd which each of the warriors carried. They were all so tired that they simply wrapped themselves in their cloaks and slept where they lay.

Long before light, they were up and off again, running like a small pack of hounds following a scent. The Somalis could not spread the cattle out enough not to leave a clear trail when they were passing over earth and sand, but when the ground was stony the tracks vanished and it became much harder. Several times they lost the trail and had to stop and cast about.

Suddenly one of the warriors gave a peculiar whoop.

'That means he has seen something,' said Saguta, who Jake always tried to stay near.

The warriors gathered round the companion, who was crouched down staring ahead. He told them he had spotted something in the distance. Being so far away it was impossible to see exactly what it was. Jake lay down beside the warrior and asked him to show him where it was. Once he had it pinpointed, he looked through his binoculars, adjusted the focus and a figure sprang into view. It appeared to be behaving strangely, weaving about, falling over and then getting up and heading in a new direction. He described this to them.

'We must be careful,' said Saguta. 'It may be a trick. You stay here and keep watch through your glasses. If you see anything suspicious give a shout.'

Cautiously the rest advanced until the figure was surrounded, when they all rushed in holding up their spears and whooping. At this, it fell down and lay still with its hands clasped over its head. They turned it over to find that it was one of the young boys. He was covered in mud and blood, scratched from head to foot by thorns and weeping piteously. It was clear that he thought his last moment had come and it took some time to calm him down.

Slowly they extracted his story from him. After the attack, he and the four other survivors had agreed that one of their number, the most injured, would return to the village and raise the alarm while the others followed the cattle. At first it had been easy. Then the Somalis had spotted one of their pursuers and after that they kept being shot at by one of the men who had waited behind in hiding. Two had been injured and had headed for home. They must have missed them on the way. That had left only him and one other still able to go on. But they had had to cover twice as much ground as the cattle, making wide sweeps through the bush in order to avoid being caught. This was how he had been so terribly scratched, as some of the hills they had climbed had been covered in thick scrub.

Eventually, he had become exhausted and dropped behind. Lost, he had been at the end of his tether when they found him. The remaining boy, whose name was Karna, was the oldest of the group and he should still be somewhere ahead. The boy they had found, who was one of the youngest, told them that the cattle were not very far ahead, but that they must be very careful if they were to avoid being shot. 'If they hide and wait with a gun it is impossible to see them until it is too late,' he explained. He was given a drink, pointed in the right direction, and told to go home.

From now on, they had to be extra careful. They did not want the raiders to know how close they were and they did not, of course, want to be shot. As a result they had to spread out even wider than before and to keep in contact by imitating the cries of various animals. Several times they had narrow escapes from dangerous encounters with animals. The area had a lot of lions; they had heard them roaring during the night. The danger was that to keep out of sight of possible watchers they had to pass through the middle of large clumps of scrub which they would normally avoid. These were exactly the places where lions and other large animals like to lie up during the day.

Twice warriors stumbled over sleeping lions and came running out of scrub to accompanying sounds of furious roars from within. Saguta said that normally his *laji* would never run away but would stay and fight the lion to the death. But now they had a more important duty, which was to get their cattle back.

'In the old days, every warrior would kill a lion,' he explained as they trotted along side by side. 'Sometimes he would do it alone if he was there when one came to kill his cattle. Usually, a group of boys would set out to follow one which had taken a cow or calf. If they found it they would all attack with their spears. The most important job is to grab the tail. If one of them can do that, he hangs on for all he's worth while the others deal with the lion. I have not been able to do that yet,' he went on looking ashamed. 'I will not consider myself a true warrior until I have.'

'Why is it so important to kill a lion?' asked Jake.

'Because it has always been so' was the answer. 'We do not kill because we enjoy it but because it is necessary to protect our cattle. Now lions are less of a threat to them than these Shifta. That is our name for these bandits who steal what is not theirs. We do not want to kill them either, but how else are we to survive?

'If we kill a lion it brings us great credit with our people. We would keep the skin to show how brave we are – and it also makes wonderful sandals for special occasions. The claws are important symbols of manhood, and they are used for jewellery, too.'

That evening they found the carcass of one of their cows. It made them all very angry. They recognized it and were incensed to see it dead. The raiders had started to butcher it for meat but had clearly been in a hurry so that not much had been taken. Once the Samburu had calmed down, they decided that they should at least benefit from their enemies' behaviour in killing a good cow, something they would never do just for meat, and have some themselves. As darkness was falling, they lit a fire and ate their fill for once before lying down for a short sleep. That night hyenas, attracted by the carcass of the cow, circled the camp and disturbed them with their bloodcurdling screams. In the morning, as they left, Jake looked back and saw the sinister creatures dashing in as soon as the last Samburu was out of spear throwing range of the dead cow. They ran in a sidling, almost apologetic, way which he found revolting, but the strength of their jaws was unmistakable. He could hear the bones being crunched long after the dreadful scene was obscured by bushes.

Jake was keeping up well with the others. He found that by staying more or less in the middle of the spread out line of warriors he did not have to travel quite so far. Also, as they ran in a sort of crescent, with the outer arms quite a lot in front, it was less likely that the centre would stumble on the raiders without any warning. It was those on the outside edges who were in the most danger. They were like scouts and it would be they who, in all likelihood, would get the first glimpse of the enemy.

They were also the ones most likely to disturb wild animals. Here Jake and his binoculars again came in useful. Whenever there was a small hill, Jake would climb it and spend some time scanning the terrain ahead for animals or people. Several times during the next day he was able to shout a warning so that they could make a detour. Nonetheless, he twice saw angry buffalo charge across the line, the Samburu who had roused them having scurried smartly out of the way. Once it was a furious rhino which charged. This thrilled Jake as he had not seen one before; until he realized, to his horror, that it seemed to be heading in his direction.

'Quick!' shouted Saguta, who was some distance from him at that moment. 'Climb a tree!'

Jake looked around desperately. Most of the trees were low thorn trees, acacias. Not only would they hardly get him out of reach of the creature, but their thorns made him hesitate. Then he saw that there was a proper big tree about a hundred yards away. He reckoned he could just make it and set off at a sprint.

Glancing back, he saw that the rhino was not far behind. Also that it had turned as he headed for the tree and was now definitely after him. He ran faster than he ever had before and soon he could hear the pounding of its hooves behind him. Not daring to look again he stared at the tree to see how he would get up. There was only one low branch and he reckoned he could just reach it and swing himself up.

Putting on a final spurt, he made a tremendous leap and felt relief flow through him as his hands locked around the branch. He swung his legs up and hooked them over just as the rhino passed underneath, almost brushing him with its back. Fortunately, it had not seen him jump and its head was held low. If it had looked up it could easily have gored him with its horn as it passed under.

Jake's relief was short lived. With a sudden crack the branch broke, depositing Jake painfully back on the ground. The rhino heard the noise, wheeled around and started back. Jake leapt to his feet. He was about to start running when he noticed that the branch had not broken off completely. It was still attached to the tree some way up but now hung right down to the ground. Now he did not need to jump; just to run up it. Of course, if he fell he would land right in the advancing rhino's path.

Once again it was close; but this time the branch held and, once he reached the main trunk, Jake was able to shin up further to safety. The rhino turned yet again and looked as though it was about to charge the tree itself; but when it saw the line of shouting Samburu charging *it* and waving their spears, it decided to take off.

They were all pleased to see Jake safe and crowded round him to look at the cut from his fall. It was not serious, although it hurt quite a lot and so they took the opportunity to have a council of war. They were all worried about what they would do when they caught up with their cattle, which must be fairly soon now. Spears against guns is an unfair contest and their only chance was to take them by surprise. But they knew it would not be easy. Brave as they were, they were only young warriors, while their enemies were experienced robbers, full grown and well armed.

13
The Blacksmith

It was one of the warriors at the end of the line who spotted the fire. It was only a tiny wisp of smoke and it was well hidden in the bush below the shoulder of a low hill, but there was no mistaking that it was fire.

'It must be them,' said Saguta. 'They must have made a detour to fool us. If we hadn't seen the smoke, we could have run right past them.'

They decided to attack there and then so as to maintain the element of surprise. It seemed unlikely the raiders would have had time to set up a trap. Creeping over the ground at high speed bent double, was difficult and Jake got left behind. Before he could catch up, he heard a shout from all the warriors and cursed himself for missing the battle. He stood up and ran straight in.

Instead of finding a pitched battle in progress, he saw a small thorn shelter, under which one man and his family were cowering.

'It's only an *ilconone*,' said Saguta as Jake

arrived, 'a man who makes metal things. What do you call him?'

'A blacksmith, I suppose,' replied Jake. 'We don't have too many of those any more in England, but there is one in my village.'

'We are a bit frightened of them as they have powerful magic and we usually try to keep away. We had better be nice to this one now as we have given him a bad fright. Anyway, it may be a good thing we've stumbled on him as we really ought to have some extra spears and knives for when we attack the Somalis.'

The blacksmith was picked up and reassured that no one was going to kill him. His children, who had been screaming, eventually calmed down and the Samburu warriors began to negotiate with him to see if he would part with any of his goods. Of course, they could not pay him but he knew where they came from and would collect a goat for each spear when he visited their village next.

Jake looked inside the shelter and was surprised to find a small forge. The fire had died down but, as soon as he understood what was wanted of him, the blacksmith was back and pumping up a roaring furnace. There were two goatskin bellows which his wife operated with her hands, blowing air through clay funnels on to charcoal, which soon became red hot. He then laid a metal rod over the heat and, gripping

93

the other end between his feet, rapidly hammered it into the shape of a spear. Fortunately, he already had several partly made spears and knives in the shelter and so was able to satisfy their needs during the day.

The Samburu decided it was worth waiting until he had finished, but some warriors were sent ahead to scout out the land. They returned in the evening to say that they had seen the great river which runs through this part of the dry bush. Saguta explained that sometimes it almost vanishes into the sand of the desert; at others it fills with water and carries a great flood into Somalia. If the Somalis could get the cattle across it, they would probably have won, as, although it was not yet their country, there were so many of their people living there that they would have lots of allies in a battle.

'Tomorrow we must try and cut them off,' he said. 'If there is a lot of water we will stand a chance. But I wish we had guns. It is not going to be easy.'

Jake had been fascinated to see how fast the blacksmith worked. He had several half made spears which he finished off for them, so that by nightfall each had an extra one. He also made sure that all their spears and knives were sharp and in good order.

In his shelter hung the blacksmith's few possessions and his wife cooked at the edge of the furnace. Jake noticed that there was a lot of silvery jewellery hanging up and he asked Saguta to ask if he might look at it. His friend translated. When the blacksmith looked up, smiled and nodded, Jake stepped across the shelter and picked some of the jewellery up. Immediately, there was a gasp from everyone present and he realized he had done something wrong.

'What's the matter?' he asked. 'I thought it was all right for me to have a look.'

'Yes, but never to step across that line.'

Jake now saw that a line had been scored in the sand next to the forge.

'All *ilconone* put a line like that across their houses. No one is allowed to cross it, ever. We believe that a serious curse will fall on anyone who does.'

'Well, I didn't mean to,' replied Jake. 'What can I do about it? Will you say I'm sorry if I have offended him.'

Saguta had a long conversation with the blacksmith and all the others present crowded round to hear what was being discussed. After what seemed an age to Jake, as everyone was looking so serious and he was beginning to believe that a dreadful curse would fall on him, Saguta spoke in English.

'He can help you, but only if you are prepared to pay him some money. Do you have any with you?'

Jake, who had felt a bit silly doing so as he had not thought it likely he would have any opportunity to spend any, admitted that he had tucked some notes into the trouser pocket of his shorts.

'What you have to do is to buy as much of his jewellery as you can. If it is enough, then he will make you a magic bracelet which will protect you from the curse of having crossed the line.'

Jake had about £5 in Kenya money on him. After much discussion and negotiation, into which everyone joined, it proved enough to buy a necklace made of several different coloured stones separated by decorated pieces of silver; and a nice silver cross of a strange design. These he thought would make good presents for Meg and his mother if he ever got back safely.

The bracelet he was given was made of twisted iron. The blacksmith heated it and adjusted the shape so that it was a tight fit around Jake's wrist. Then, laughing, he dragged Jake backwards and forwards across the line to show that he could now do so safely.

That night, as they all camped around the blacksmith's shelter, they sat up and told stories. It seemed likely there would be a fight the next day and the warriors vied with each other to describe how brave they were going to be. If he had not known how brave they really were, Jake would have thought they were boasting – and, of course, so they were. But in their case he felt sure that, when put to the test, they would be every bit as brave as they claimed.

His own feelings were quite different. While he was caught up in the excitement of the chase and the confidence of the young Samburu, he also knew that deep down inside he was very frightened. He couldn't see how they could avoid something pretty horrible happening and he was afraid for them and for himself. In all his previous adventures he had never been badly hurt, but now he had seen the dead body of the young man who had been murdered and the same men who had done that were waiting to shoot at him. There were moments when he woke up in the night terrified at what lay ahead. At those times he would have liked to return to the sanctuary of the Safari lodge and spend the rest of his holiday just looking at all the African wildlife from the safety of a vehicle. But he knew it was too late now to turn back. Some of the Samburu heroism must have rubbed off on him when he put on their robes and when with them he felt ready for anything.

14
The River

By first light they had reached the banks of the river, which Jake now learned was called the Ewaso Ngiro. To their relief, it was running in flood and would be difficult or impossible to cross.

'It must be raining up in the mountains,' explained Saguta. 'It almost never rains down here, but the floods come from up in the hills. Now we must find where they are hiding with our cattle.'

They suspected that the Somalis would be waiting on the bank for the water level to drop, so that they could drive the cattle across. But they did not know whether they were upstream or down. With the detour to the blacksmith, they had lost the trail.

'We have decided to divide up, some going to the left, some to the right. When one group finds our enemies they will send word to the other. Only when we are all together will we attack. We must be very careful or it will not be a surprise. They know we are behind them I am sure but they may not know how far. We have seen no signs left by Karna for some time and we are afraid he may have been captured. If he had been killed, I think we would have found his body.'

Jake felt the now familiar chill of fear run up his spine. 'What signs?' he asked. 'I have seen no signs.'

'You wouldn't,' said Saguta, making Jake feel very young and inexperienced again. 'You wouldn't know what to look for. We have our own ways of signalling which people who are not Samburu would not understand. We bend over a twig, make small marks on it and leave it caught in another. We leave signs in the sand, too, which others would believe to be animal tracks, but which we all can read. Karna has been doing well, but yesterday they stopped. I am worried about him. He is my brother.'

Jake was amazed. Saguta had made no mention of a brother and he had not seemed more worried about the fate of Karna than of any of the other boys.

'What can we do?' he asked.

'Nothing at the moment. We must wait until the time is right to attack. Then we must hope that they have not killed him.'

Jake wondered how he would feel if he had a brother who might have just been captured and killed. It seemed as if Saguta was being callous, and yet if Karna was still alive the best way to save him would be to stay calm.

It was decided that Saguta's party, which of course included Jake, would go downstream while the other group turned left, upstream. If they had not found signs of their cattle or the enemy by the end of the first day, they would come back through the night to meet again at the same place the next morning.

Saguta and Jake jogged along beside the river. The rest of their small group spread out inland in case the Somalis were keeping the cattle back from the bank. There was much more vegetation here and it was far lusher than anything they had seen on the way. In some places there was thick forest, in others groves of palm trees, and sometimes the banks were just bare rocks or sand. With so much water to hand they did not have to go thirsty and some of the trees bore fruit which Saguta told Jake were edible. They were able to cover the ground fast, but by afternoon Saguta was looking worried again.

'It looks to me as though the river is dropping,' he replied when Jake asked him what was wrong. 'It rises and falls very quickly, so we may not have much time before it is shallow enough to drive our cattle across.'

They ran on for a while, and then Saguta

stopped so suddenly that Jake almost crashed into him.

'What is it?' he whispered, as Saguta was standing stock still and listening.

Without answering, his friend began to walk very slowly and carefully towards the clump of bushes they were passing. Jake remained where he was, hardly daring to breath. When he reached the first bush, having not made a sound, Saguta gently parted the branches and looked into the space behind. For a moment he stood with his spear raised, then he lowered it and knelt down. Jake hurried over and together they lifted the body of a young Samburu out into the open.

'Is it Karna?' Jake asked and the other nodded.

'I think he is alive, but he is badly hurt. Could you bring some water from the river.'

When they had bathed the boy's face and washed his wounds, which did not seem to be too deep, they watched as his eyes began to flicker and he started to mumble. Suddenly he sat up and tried to hit them but Saguta caught his wrist and began to speak reassuringly. Gradually, recognition dawned and then, slowly at first but gathering speed and urgency, Karna began to speak.

At last Saguta turned to Jake. 'He says that the Shifta are quite close and we must be very careful. They have guns and they are good shots. They ambushed him yesterday and beat him up but they did not shoot him as they said they would take him with them and sell him as a slave. He managed to escape in the night, but one of them followed and caught up with him at dawn. That is when he was wounded as the man had a spear and his own had been taken from him. Luckily the Somali was distracted by some hippos returning to the river and he was able to crawl away into the bushes.

At that moment a shot rang out. Both boys dropped to the ground at once beside Karna, imagining that it was aimed at them. They lay still and then there was another shot. Peering cautiously through the rushes which hid them from view, they saw a Somali man with a rifle step out of the forest and look down at the river. Out on a sandbank lay the body of a large crocodile, still lashing its tail from side to side, but clearly dying.

'We never kill crocodiles,' whispered Saguta. 'They are not good to eat and we believe that if we do them no harm they will leave us alone. It doesn't always work,' he added with a grin, much more cheerful now the enemy was in sight. But these Shifta will kill anything they can get money for. He will sell the skin.'

Sure enough, the Somali climbed down the bank, waded through the shallows to the sandbank and, using a vicious looking knife he took from his belt, began to skin his prey.

'I'm going to try and get his gun,' whispered Saguta. 'I can run across from the bank and grab it.'

The gun was lying propped against some driftwood about five metres from the Somali, who was now covered in blood up to his elbows.

'You'll never get there before he sees you,' Jake advised. 'We are going to have to make a better plan. Do you know how to shoot that kind of gun? It looks strange to me and I don't think I would know what to do. If you got there and couldn't shoot you would be in real trouble. He probably has friends within earshot on the bank. I don't think we should try anything until the rest have arrived and we can attack the force.'

'I must have that gun,' insisted Saguta in a voice which Jake recognized meant that he would go for it whether he had help or not.

'If I help you to get it will you promise not to do anything else until the rest arrive? I have a plan and I think I can distract him. Also, you should stay here and look after your brother until he is able to walk.'

'Okay, but what do you suggest?' asked Saguta, who was ready to do something desperate but understood the sense of what Jake was suggesting.

'How about if I float past on the other side of

the sandbank. I can then attract his attention so that he will be looking in my direction and that will give you more time to work out how to use the gun. There will also be two of us to tackle him if need be. I will take my spears with me.'

They crept back upstream for a few yards and slid down the bank to the water's edge. A large log lay conveniently on the sand. When they rolled it into the river it floated high out of the water. There was even half a branch on one side, to which Jake could cling and so lie out of sight.

'Wait until you see me passing before you make your run. And good luck!' Jake whispered and pushed off into the stream. As soon as he did so he began to realize that he might have made a big mistake. The current was much faster than he had expected and the log took off at high speed. It was impossible to control and there were small waves which buffeted it about.

He gripped the branch and lay half sub-merged, holding his breath when the log rolled and his head went under the water. It was then that it occurred to him that where there was one crocodile there were certainly more. 'I must be mad,' he thought. But there had been so little time to make a proper plan if they were to get the Somali's gun before he finished skinning his crocodile.

Peering over the log, Jake saw that his plan

was not going so badly. He could see the sand-bank with the crouched figure on it ahead and it looked as though he would pass on the far side within about twenty metres of the man. He could not see Saguta, but knew where he would be. There was a convenient clump of bushes below the bank, plenty of cover to hide some-one.

As he drew level with the Somali he poked his head over the log and whistled. The man looked up from his work and stared in amazement for a second . . . but only for a second. Quick as a flash, he had sprung, almost in a single bound, to the log, grabbed his gun and run back to the edge of the sandbank nearest to Jake. He started shooting and Jake could hear the bullets whistling over his head and thudding into the log. He did his best to stay on the far side, but it kept rolling and giving the gunman another chance.

The current was beginning to take the log along even faster, but for some reason this had the effect of turning it so that Jake was spread-eagled on top. He looked despairingly towards his would-be assassin and saw that this time he was taking careful aim. But he also saw that a lean dark figure was running up behind him with a spear held high and about to strike. The shot and the jolt as the log hit a rock came together and Jake's first thought was that he had been hit. Then he found that he had been jerked off the log into the water, that nothing hurt but he was having to swim for his life.

Without noticing, he had started down some steep rapids and there was now no way he could swim to the shore. It was all he could do to stay afloat and he was going faster and faster. There was a roaring sound ahead and he realized with a terrified shudder that it must be coming from a waterfall. He tried desperately to swim against the current but it was hopeless and the next thing he knew he was falling through space.

15
Escape

He was drowning. There was water everywhere:
above and below and all around. He would
never breathe sweet air again. The water was
green, then brown, then white. White! White
water! That meant water breaking in the air.
Air! It must be somewhere near. With a huge
effort, Jake made himself strike out with something like a swimming stroke – and a moment
later his head shot out of the water.

He took a great gulp of air and tried to swim
further. But he found the current was still too
strong and that he had barely enough strength
left to keep himself afloat now he had reached
the surface. He did not want to go down into the
depths again and so contented himself with
spreading his arms out and paddling as the current swept him along.

In time it began to seem as though things were
slowing down. Now he could swim across the
current and soon his feet struck the bottom.
Gasping and spluttering, he hauled himself up

the bank and collapsed on some hot, dry rocks. The warmth of the sun was wonderful and he soon began to feel better, but he still lay there, revelling in simply being alive.

Reluctantly, he stood up after a while and took stock of his situation. He reckoned that he had travelled a fair way down the stream, and he had landed back on the same bank. Apart from that he hadn't a clue where he was. He seemed not to have hurt himself crashing through all those rapids, but every inch of his body ached and he felt desperately tired. He had lost his spears and his *rungu*, but his dagger was still tied to his belt and his trainers were still on his feet. The binoculars were still around his neck but his *shuka* had been torn from his shoulders so that all he was dressed in was his shorts. All he had in the pockets were his Swiss Army knife and the jewellery he had bought from the blacksmith. 'Things could be worse,' he thought as he took them off and laid them out to dry on the rocks. 'But I'm going to be very cold when it gets dark.'

It was a pretty spot where he had landed. There were tall trees on the opposite bank and a pile of rocks on his side. As he watched, a herd of elephants came down to the water on the far side and began to drink. Jake felt that he was invisible and lay still watching them, fascinated. He knew something about Indian elephants,* but these were his first African ones. His first impression was how much bigger they were. The half dozen adult females in the herd were huge and they had much bigger ears, too, which they constantly flapped to keep away the flies. With them were several babies which rushed into the water and started to play. They butted each other head on and then one would chase another in and out of the adults' legs until they reached a deeper hole when both would flop into the water and roll about. They were so clearly having fun that Jake had to stop himself laughing aloud and alerting them to his presence.

With time to think as he lay hidden behind a rock and waited for the elephants to move on, he began to worry about Saguta. He had promised that he would not attack until the others arrived. If all had gone well, his friend would have managed to overcome the Somali and take his gun. Then he would have had to find the rest of his group and send one back to fetch the other group, while he waited with his young brother. That would take at least a day and a night, meaning that the attack would not happen until the following evening at the earliest. He wanted to be there to help, as he was very much afraid that the *Imurran* would simply rush in against the

*Jake's Treasure

Somali guns and be in danger of being massacred if their ploy went wrong. They were undoubtedly great fighters, but the Somalis would be expecting them. There must be a better way of tricking them and getting the cattle back.

Jake also hoped that the Somali camp was far enough away from the river for them not to have heard the shots. That would have brought them running, unless they thought their companion was simply blasting off at more crocodiles when he had been shooting at Jake and the log.

He lay in the last of the sun thinking until he was rested, the elephants had left and his shorts were dry. Putting them on, he started walking back upstream to look for his friends. He could see that the river made a big curve and decided that he would save time by cutting the corner. He therefore left the bank and set off towards a hill behind which the sun was setting.

It was pleasantly cool walking in the dark, but it became more and more frightening as his ears became accustomed to the night noises. The night was clear and the stars were very bright, but there was no moon and everything around him was black. The horizon was hard to see and the hill disappeared as the contour of the land changed. He thought he had better try navigating by the stars and looked around to see if he could see any familiar ones. His father had taught him how to find the Pole Star by looking at the Plough, but as he was practically on the equator he could not see that. The only constellation he recognized was Orion's Belt which was low in the sky but gave him a bearing of sorts.

He hurried on, walking as fast as he could. Rocks and bushes loomed up in front of him. They kept looking just like animals, and sometimes they were. He stumbled right into the middle of a herd of sleeping antelope which leapt to their feet snorting and charged off in all directions. One practically knocked him flying as it brushed past him in its panic.

There were more sinister noises, too. Lions were roaring, jackals yelped and he was sure he heard the cough of a leopard. Saguta had described how cunning leopards were and how they hunted at night. He became convinced that one was following him. Then he heard the bloodcurdling laughing cry of hyenas. They were ahead of him and from the noise he assumed they were fighting over a kill. He was tempted to make a detour round them but was sure that he would then get lost, and so he trudged on.

The dreadful noises came closer and closer until he thought he was going to walk right in among them. Then he was level with the kill and he could even see vague shapes flitting about in the darkness. He thought he was past when, all of a sudden and with no warning, the yapping and shrieking stopped. For a while there was absolute silence, as if the whole bush was waiting to see what would happen next. Jake could feel them staring towards him and he, too, stood motionless, listening.

The silence seemed to go on for ever. Then, just as he was considering starting to walk again, there was a loud shriek right beside him, which made him almost jump out of his skin. He yelled out as well, which, when he thought about it later, probably saved his life as it must have scared the hyena as much as its shriek had terrified him.

In a panic, he started to run; blindly, but as fast as he could; anywhere, just to get away from those terrifying creatures. Fortunately, he was in relatively open country and he was able to keep up a good speed. He was convinced that the pack was just behind him and fear kept him going long after he would normally have stopped to catch his breath. Now bushes seemed to reach out to grab him as he passed. Thorns grazed and scratched him and several times he stumbled and fell sprawling on the ground. However much it hurt he could not stop but had to scramble up and run on, panting now with fear and exhaustion.

He must have run for an hour, before, seeing a pile of rocks ahead of him, he climbed frantically to the top and collapsed. If they followed him up there, he could at least make a proper last stand. He drew his short sword and waited for them to come.

Nothing happened. He listened and found that all was still except for the pounding of his heart. He tried to remember when he had last actually heard his pursuers. Had he really heard them at all; or had it all been in his imagination? He could not have outrun them. Hyenas, he believed, never gave up once they had started to hunt something. With a sense of relief, but also some embarrassment, he concluded that they had probably never even started chasing him.

He also realized he was completely lost. Orion's Belt was nowhere to be seen. It had either dropped below the horizon or it was obscured by the high clouds which now covered part of the sky. Dawn could not be very far off and he decided to get some rest, since in any case he felt too tired to carry on walking. The rock was still warm from the previous day's sun and so he stretched out and slept.

16
Rescue

Lying on his rock above the plain Jake dreamt. It was a confused dream in which lots of things he had been worrying about were all jumbled together.

Meg, who seemed to have turned into a cow, was being chased by men with sticks. He had to save her but he was running through deep sand and he could not keep up. The men were grinning and confident. They were firing guns which made a strange squeak each time they went off instead of a bang. Their targets were tall Samburu boys, who stood negligently on one leg and did not try to dodge the bullets. They were painted and decorated beautifully with red ochre, but Jake could see that it was turning to blood and beginning to ooze down their bodies. He tried to shout and warn them but they just gazed into the distance.

Waking, he slowly opened his eyes. The most hideous face he had ever seen was staring straight into his. Convinced that he must still be dreaming, he closed his eyes again and then, very slowly opened them again. He was not dreaming.

The face was almost human, but not really. Little angry eyes, close together above a dog-like nose, were staring straight into his. The face was red and framed by a dramatic mane of almost white hair, which grew down over the cheeks like old-fashioned whiskers and made whatever it was look like a distinguished but furious old man. It was not a man.

Closing his eyes again, Jake wondered what to do. He could try a gentle approach, reason with it and make friends, but the look in those eyes had not been encouraging. Or he could do what he had when scared by the hyenas. That had worked.

Without warning, and almost before he had made his mind up, he shouted at the top of his voice and leapt to his feet. The monkey (Jake guessed it was some sort of baboon) fell over backwards and scrambled off down the rocks shrieking. A whole troop of females and young came out of hiding and raced off behind it. Feeling like Tarzan, but shaking with fear at what would have happened if his ploy had not worked since the animal could easily have torn him apart, Jake thumped his chest and gave another loud shout. However, he decided that if they wanted their rocks back they could have them and he was not going to fight them for possession.

He scrambled down the far side from the baboons and jogged off with the rising sun on his back. Now he was thirsty. He had not had a drink since leaving the river and he would be in trouble if he did not find some water soon. The scrubby landscape around did not look promising; he must try and get back to the river. That, after all, was where his companions were. The problem was that he had lost his bearings and only knew that he had set off the night before heading west. In between, as he charged about running away from the hyenas he could have gone anywhere.

For four hours he hurried on without seeing any sign of the river. By mid-day he was in a bad way. His tongue was dry; his body, already badly scratched from his adventures in the night, was now becoming painfully sunburnt; and his legs were beginning to give out. If he didn't find something or someone soon he would be in deep trouble.

He dare not stop as he had to reach the others before the battle. It did not occur to him that if he did stumble on them he would be more of a liability than an asset. Nor did he consider that he was just as likely to wander into the Somali camp. All he knew was that he had to keep going.

As the heat beat down on his head he began to become delirious. He started talking to himself, but because his mouth was so dry it came out as a mad mumble. He could no longer remember what he was looking for but wanted to find anything that was not just sand and scrub. As he came over a low ridge he saw something different away ahead. He could not tell what it was, but it was certainly different. It was a flashing light, but that was impossible in the daytime. It was so strong it dazzled him. His brain was too confused to work out what it might be; all he knew was that he must reach it, and he began to run in its direction.

For a while his mind blanked out and he was aware of neither pain nor thirst nor fear. But his body kept going towards the flashing light until he got there. He awoke to find himself in paradise and thought for one lucid moment that, instead of dreaming, this time he must have died.

In front of him was a table with a huge jug of water on it. Ice floated on the surface and there were tall glasses beside it. There was a bowl of fresh fruit, glistening with dewdrops, and, before he collapsed to the ground, Jake saw that there was even a fresh white tablecloth.

The Italian film crew, who had stopped for lunch, were as surprised as Jake when a ragged, shirtless boy covered in scratches staggered into their camp and fell to the ground. They gathered round him solicitously, pouring water over his face and through his lips until he spluttered and came round. He opened his eyes and thought for a moment that time was playing tricks on him. The face peering into his was red and framed with a shock of white hair. Until his eyes focused, it could have been the baboon come back to haunt him. Then he saw that this face had kind eyes and was speaking to him.

'I saw a light,' were Jake's first words. 'What was it?'

Solving this problem broke the ice and everyone discussed how he could have found them and what he must have seen, until someone pointed at the satellite disc above the camp, which caught the sun and reflected it into the distance.

'What are you all doing here?' Jake asked.

'Making a film about Africa. We have only flown in for the day and we will be leaving soon. You are very lucky to have found us. Now tell us what *you* are doing.'

Jake told his story and they all listened eagerly. There were five of them, including two Kenyan pilots, and they all spoke English. 'So you see,' Jake concluded, 'I really am desperate to help my friends. They will be killed if we don't do something.'

The Director was a tall, grey haired man. It

was he who had reminded Jake of the baboon. He told Jake to lie and rest while he went off to talk to the pilots. 'How are we off for fuel?' Jake heard him ask as they walked out of earshot.

'You need some food,' said a voice. 'Don't worry about anything. Our Direttore will fix everything. My name is Luigi and I am the cameraman. Sit at the table now and relax.'

Jake did as he was told, while the Italian described the film they were making. It was an adventure story about big game hunting set in the 1930s. 'Our hero crashes in the bush after an encounter with poachers. We are nearly finished, but perhaps your story will give the Direttore some new ideas. He keeps on changing the plot!'

Jake was almost too busy to listen as he tucked into a meal of fresh eggs, pasta and fruit. It was a long time since he had tasted anything so delicious.

'Where does all this food come from?' he asked.

'We only flew here early this morning from a little place called Lipi and we're going back tonight. There is an old airstrip near here where we were able to land. We carried the icebox over here because it's nice and shady. We also had to put up the disc so as to stay in touch with the other crews who are working in different places.'

'Do you think I could have a lift?' asked Jake,

hardly daring to believe his luck. 'My aunt lives there, but I can't possibly go until the cattle are rescued . . .' he added.

At that moment the Director returned. 'Are you sure that your friends are going to attack these robbers soon?' he asked.

'Definitely,' Jake replied. 'As soon as they are all together they will rush in and I am very much afraid that they will be killed. They love their cattle more than life itself and they are desperate to stop them being driven across the river.'

'Well my brave young friend, I have a plan. We are about to fly back to Lipi, but my pilots tell me they have plenty of spare fuel. I need some extra film to do with poachers and I have thought of a story we could add into our little plot. Our hero is fighting against poachers and he has an aeroplane. It is only logical that at some point he will attack them from the air. Do you understand what I am suggesting and do you think it will work?'

Jake got it at once and thought it brilliant. His only question was 'How am I going to let them know that it's me? If they don't understand what we're doing we may make things worse.'

'We will take off one of the doors and you can sit where your friends can see you. There will be no chance of landing again once we have taken off, so we'll have to leave them to it.'

'Well, let's get on with it,' said Jake eagerly.

'We mustn't leave it too late.'

The planes were soon loaded up and ready for take-off. The Director took Jake on one side. 'I want you to fly with me in one plane; Luigi will be in the other and will be filming us for my story. We can talk to each other by radio but you will have to identify what is going on. We only have ten or fifteen minutes extra time to do whatever we decide must be done. Then we will have to fly back to Lipi. Is that okay with you?'

'Yes, it sounds great,' replied Jake. 'Only, I will have to lean right out. Will I be safe?'

'No problem. You will be so well strapped in that you could fall out and still be safe,' answered the Director, and he slapped Jake on his back, which hurt. 'Don't worry. I'm not going to lose you now! I have explained to the pilot what we are trying to do.'

Jake was put in the front seat of the smaller plane, on the right of the pilot. The door had been removed. The pilot's name was Jim. He leaned across and whispered to Jake before starting the engines. 'I don't know how you persuaded the Boss to do this. We're breaking every rule in the book. But he's paying so . . .'

They took off and were soon flying up the river. Soon Jake saw the rapids he had been swept over. They did not look nearly as impressive from the air as they had when he was in the water. Moreover, the water had dropped a lot and there were many more sandbanks. He asked Jim to turn and drop down to search the bush.

They found the cattle almost at once. They were hidden from all directions except the air, being penned in a small valley between two low hills. Beside them he could see the Somalis' camp. 'Can you drop even lower and see if we can find my Samburu friends?' he asked.

'Sure,' said Jim. 'This little plane can do anything. I'll just tell the other lot to hang around until we call them. With two engines they are much less manoeuvrable.'

Practically skimming the tops of the acacia trees and flying as slowly as possible, they began to circle out from the cattle. It was Jake who spotted the Samburu first. Although they were trying to hide in the next valley, just below the ridge, their red cloaks stood out from the air and Jake gave a whoop. It looked as though they were assessing their enemies before attacking.

'Can we try and let them know I'm on board now?' he asked, and immediately Jim swung the plane over on to its side. Jake would have fallen out if he had not been so well strapped in, but he hung out as far as he could feeling the strong rush of air pasts his face. He was able to get one arm up in the air and with this he waved for all he was worth as they skimmed over the warriors. He saw them look up and he could pick out

Saguta. He was sure he had recognized him and he had also done a quick count and reckoned that the two groups must have joined up.

'Now we can lead the attack,' Jake told Jim. 'They will know what to do if we make a start.'

The two aircraft circled around to the head of the valley and then came down it as low as possible, one behind the other. Jake's plane was first and the wind of its passing stirred up dust around the cattle as it passed right above their heads. They surged against the temporary fence the Somalis had erected, but it held. Then came the second plane and this time they panicked. The noise was much louder; they milled around their small compound once; then charged the fence and broke through. The Somalis could be seen running around frantically trying to drive them back in.

'They still don't know what's happening,' he said into the microphone. 'Let's show them.'

Jim wheeled steeply around, gained some height and then divebombed the valley. This time it was the Somalis who scattered. The plane seemed to be coming straight at them. They forgot the cattle and started running for the river. The country they were crossing was bare of trees, which meant that the planes could go even lower. They ran, still clutching their rifles. One of them stopped and, turning, knelt to take aim at the plane.

Again Jim gained a little height. Just as he was at the top and about to dive, Jake saw a tiny puff come from the barrel and at the same moment there was a ping as a bullet hit the fuselage.

'Right!' shouted Jim into the radio. 'If that's the way you want it, here goes' and he went into another steep dive straight at the bandit. This time Jake thought they were going to fly into the ground. He could see the gun and it was pointing directly at them.

At the last possible moment Jim pulled out of the dive. But by then the bandit had started to run after his friends. Now the Samburu came over the hill and charged down towards the fugitives waving their spears. Although he could not hear them, Jake was sure that they would be shouting at the tops of their voices and he was not surprised to see the Somalis run even faster.

They only had time for one more circuit before the pilots said they must start for Lipi. The two planes flew side by side down the river just as the last figure leapt off the bank a few yards in front of his pursuers and started to swim across. They turned and came back upstream. Now the Samburu were clustered on the bank and they seemed to be doing a war dance. The planes waggled their wings as they passed over them and all the spears were raised in a salute.

'I don't expect those robbers will try again for

some time,' said the Director with a smile. 'If they made it past the crocodiles, that is!'

Sitting back in his seat, Jake gave a deep sigh of contentment as he looked down and saw the barren country he had walked across whizz past. 'This is the way to travel,' he thought. 'My only problem now is to think what to tell Meg.'

Epilogue

To his relief, Jake found that Meg was still away, although she was expected back at any moment. He was able to have a good bath, get his clothes washed and generally smarten himself up. Even Meg would, he felt, have been shocked to see him in the state in which he arrived back. He was covered in scratches, his clothes were in rags, his skin started to peel badly, and he had not washed for well over a week.

The Italians had made themselves very comfortable in a well equipped camp outside the town and they sent a car to fetch him in the evening. They feasted and told stories about the adventures of the day until the whole incident had grown into the stuff of legends. They were leaving in the morning and they made Jake promise to write and tell them how it had all worked out. The Director was especially pleased as he said that his film now had the perfect climax.

'You must watch out for it,' he told Jake. 'It

will be called *The Disaster Safari* in English and I will see that your name appears in the credits for having provided Special Effects!'

Meg arrived later in the morning to catch Jake still in bed. 'Well, you are a lazy old thing,' she told him as she shook him awake. 'I am sorry to have been away so long. It was all a bit of a problem, but it's sorted out now. I do hope you haven't been too bored.'

'Not exactly,' Jake replied, looking her straight in the eye. 'Can you keep a secret?'

Meg, who had only just noticed, as he sat up in bed, just how sunburnt and scratched his body was, went very still, sat down on the bed and said,

'Jake, you've been up to something, haven't you, and I have a horrible feeling that I shouldn't have left you. Are you all right? If anything had happened to you I would never have forgiven myself – and your mother would have killed me. You had better tell me all about it.'

Jake told her the whole story while she watched him and listened without interrupting except to mutter once or twice 'You idiot!' But whether she was referring to what Jake had been doing or to her own stupidity in allowing him off on his own Jake never knew.

When he had finished, she gave him a big hug and said, 'I've never had any secrets from your mother, who is my best friend, but I think this is

127

one story we'll keep to ourselves, don't you? Now, I've got to do a quick round of the clinic to make sure everything's under control, then you and I are going to get ready for a real holiday. We'll go back to the Wilsons and stay there for a whole week. That should provide you with plenty to tell your mother when you get home.'

Dick and Jenny Wilson were delighted to have them back. 'Well done!' Dick whispered to Jake as they carried their bags in. 'What on earth did you do to persuade her to take a holiday?'

'It was quite hard,' replied Jake with a secret grin.

Joseph welcomed Jake solemnly and said at once, 'So you have come back to learn how to drive, have you?'

'Oh yes, please,' answered Jake enthusiastically, and he had his first lesson right away. Within a couple of days he was being allowed to do some of the driving for tour groups, so that Joseph could stand up and identify the wildlife even better. They even went on a couple of night Safaris. Then Jake controlled a powerful torch mounted on the roof, directing it at animals which he was able to locate by their eyes shining in the light. 'Just remember that leopards have green eyes and are better not provoked,' was Joseph's advice.

The days passed happily and his memories of his adventures with the Samburu were already beginning to fade when Meg told him it was time to go back to Lipi for a couple of days before he caught his flight home.

'You must come back any time,' Dick told him as they left. 'I can't tell you how grateful we are to you for dragging Meg down here. It's probably the longest holiday she's ever taken. And Joseph says you're a star with the tourists. If you ever need a job, there's one here for you.'

'I might just take you up on that one day,' said Jake, and he meant it. He could think of nothing he'd rather do than earn his living watching and learning more and more about the wonderful wildlife of Africa.

'Not yet you don't, my boy,' said Meg pushing him into the Land Rover. 'I promised your mother I'd get you safely back to school,' and Jake made a face as he waved the Wilsons good-bye.

Saguta's *nkang* was quiet as Jake walked down the hill towards it. Meg understood that he had to go back and see his friends again and, after what he had been through with them, she could hardly insist that he needed company on the way there. And so he had taken the bus and walked in from the road alone.

It was good to be back in the dry scrub. The sounds were familiar now and much less frightening. But he still kept a watchful eye out for danger. As his nostrils picked up the rich smell of woodsmoke from the fires inside the enclosure, he began to hear the contented sounds of Samburu life. Goats bleated, children laughed and someone was beating a piece of metal.

Saguta's mother ran over and clasped him in her arms when she saw him. 'A very un-Samburu thing to do,' thought Jake. Her husband shook his hand gravely and said 'Thanks to you our son Karna is now well. You helped to save him. Also all our cattle are now safely back.'

'Where is Saguta?' asked Jake.

'Not far away. He is with his *laji*. Karna will show you. He is strong enough now.'

Karna grinned at Jake as they trotted along together. His wounds had healed and he was looking forward to getting back to the cattle. On the way he told Jake what had happened after he had floated off down the river.

'Saguta speared the Shifta before he could shoot you and he took the rifle. 'Unfortunately there were no more bullets. He had used them all up trying to kill you. The others arrived the next day and we were just preparing to attack when we heard the planes overhead. At first we were frightened, but then we saw you leaning out of the side and we were astonished. And when you drove the cattle to escape and then chased the Shifta to the river the others all ran after them; only I had to stay behind because I was wounded. But I saw it all from the hill. It was wonderful; the best battle ever.

'Then we drove the cattle back home. I was very ill and they made a stretcher and carried me. But I am better now. The elders are very happy that we got the cattle back. They have given Saguta a copper bracelet.'

'What is that for?' asked Jake.

'It is a great honour. It is only given to warriors who have been very brave and killed an enemy.'

'A bit like the VC, I suppose,' thought Jake. 'Well, I certainly don't know anyone braver than my Samburu friends.'

This time, as they neared the warriors' camp, Jake was able to smell the cows. They stopped on a little rise and, for a moment, Jake was able to watch the still form of the Samburu warrior below him, standing motionless on one leg watching over his beloved cows. He knew it was Saguta before he turned, smiled his recognition, and walked towards him.

'So you have come back,' he said as greeting.

'Only for today, I'm afraid. I have to go back to school and my flight is tomorrow evening.'

'Me too,' replied Saguta. 'I am soon going to have to leave my *laji* and go back to Lipi for another term. I like it better here but my father says I must learn to fight with words as well as spears.'

'You are a great warrior now, I see,' said Jake pointing at the copper bracelet on his friend's wrist. 'You see, I am beginning to learn about Samburu ways! You are famous.'

'Not as famous as you. Already they are making songs about how you flew to our help. Of course, we could easily have done it without you.'

The boys smiled conspiratorially at each other. Both knew what a close thing it had been but, for different reasons, both also knew that it was better to pretend that it had been easy.

'You are going to have to keep a sharp eye out for trouble in the future as I expect they'll be back one day. Here, I would like you to have these,' and he took the binoculars off his neck and gave them to Saguta.

'Thank you, my friend. I will use them to protect my cattle, but also to look out for you so that I see you from a long way off when you are coming back. Please come back soon. We will be waiting.'

❖ Tales of Redwall ❖
BRIAN JACQUES

'Not since Roald Dahl have children filled their shelves so compulsively' *The Times*

An award-winning, best-selling series from master storyteller, Brian Jacques. Discover the epic Tales of Redwall adventures about Redwall Abbey - and beyond!

Redwall Map and Riddler
BRIAN JACQUES

Get ready to take the Redwall Map and Riddler challenge - it's the ultimate Redwall adventure!

The **Redwall Map** is a perfect reading companion for all fans - old and new - of the legendary **Tales of Redwall** by Brian Jacques. Beautifully illustrated in full colour, it lavishly charts all the places, landmarks and sites made famous by the Redwall stories.

And there's more!

With the map comes **The Redwall Riddler**, a quiz book crammed full of riddles to unravel, quick-fire questions, baffling word puzzles and cryptic conundrums. So now you can test your Redwall know-how with tricky brain-teasers like these:

✡ In REDWALL, Cluny the Scourge only has one eye. How is he reputed to have lost the other?

Answer:

✡ In battle with a pike

Redwall Map and Riddler by Brian Jacques
Red Fox, £4.99 ISBN 0 09 925611 8

LOCH

*P*aul Zindel's blood-chilling thriller is out now – grab a copy for the most terrifying roller-coaster read of your life.

Here's a taster to get you trembling...

The explosion from the water came quickly. The camera fell from Erdon's hands as he glimpsed a pair of huge, horrifying yellow eyes and a gorge rimmed by jagged, dagger-sized teeth. The horror happened so fast – as if Erdon had been struck by the hood of a racing car, his feet torn from the rope webbing – he had an instant to feel the impact on his face and chest. He was aware of a brief sensation of being turned, positioned, when a godless, fiery pain crashed simultaneously into his back and groin.

At first, Sarah didn't have time to scream. Instinctively, she reached for the ignition key, but as her arm and hand went out she felt warm, thick drops spotting her skin. When she looked at her arm she knew it was raining blood. Now she screamed.

RED FOX *paperback*, £2.99 ISBN 0 09 954261 7
THE BODLEY HEAD *hardback*, £8.99 ISBN 0370 324307

THE DOOM STONE

WARNING!!! This is a grippingly gory, adrenaline-pumping, non-stop-action block-buster of a read...

A deadly predator is stalking Salisbury Plain, leaving a blood-curdling legacy of terror, murder and destruction in its wake. This killing machine must be stopped before it kills again – and again.

In the next split second Richards glimpsed an enormous skull-like face with horrifying, deep, huge eye sockets. The impact ripped his legs from the ladder and hurled his body against the ceiling beams. He was aware of being turned by great clawed hands locking him like pincers, and he was ashamed to find himself screaming. He stared helplessly down into the skull-face, saw it open its mouth. A huge, gnashing spray of twisted, razor-sharp fangs spiralled upwards and began to penetrate his throat. He felt a deep unspeakable pain, saw the burst of his own blood in front of him. In his last conscious moments on earth, he knew he was being devoured alive.

RED FOX *paperback*, £3.50 ISBN 0 09 954271 4
THE BODLEY HEAD *hardback*, £8.99 ISBN 0 37 032281 9

Book **1** in the FELIX TRILOGY

GO SADDLE THE SEA

*A*ction-packed adventure, high-tension drama and heroic swashbuckling!
Join dashing hero Felix Brooke as he boldly embarks upon the journey of a lifetime...
Here's a taster to tempt you!

'Ye've run yourself into a real nest of adders, here, lad,' Sammy whispered.

'I know they are smugglers,' I began protesting. 'That was why the fee was low. But I could take care of my — '

'They are worse than smugglers, lad – they are Comprachicos,' he breathed into my ear.

'Compra — c-comprachicos?'

At first I thought I could not have heard him aright. Then I could not believe him. The I *did* believe him – Sam would not make up such a tale – and, despite myself, my teeth began to chatter.

ANN COBURN

*B*e warned: where the edges of past and present merge and the borders of time blur... expect the unexpected.

Four very different buddies: Alice, Frankie, David and Michael, have one thing in common - photography. But their passion for cameras is developing into a very dangerous hobby...

❶ WORM SONGS   ISBN 0 09 964311 1   £2.99

❷ WEB WEAVER   ISBN 0 09 964321 9   £3.50

❸ *And coming soon!* DARK WATER   ISBN 0 09 964331 6   £3.50

THE BORDERLANDS SEQUENCE by Ann Coburn
Out now in paperback from Red Fox

THE SNOW-WALKER
SEQUENCE

Book 1

CATHERINE FISHER

THE SNOW-WALKER'S SON

Short-listed for the WH Smith Mind Boggling Books Award

Some say he's a monster, others hope he is dead, and no one has seen him for many, many years. Until now...

'I'm sending you to live with my son,' the Jarl said.

For a moment they couldn't realize what he meant. Then Jessa felt sick; cold sweat prickled on her back.

Thorkil was white. 'You can't send us there,' he breathed.

'Hold your tongue and let me finish.' Ragnar was looking at them now, with a hard, amused stare.

'Call it exile, and think yourselves lucky. At least you'll have a sort of life. You leave tomorrow for Thrasirshall, at first light.'

Jessa saw Thorkil was trembling. She knew he couldn't believe this; he was terrified. It burst out of him in a wild despairing cry.

'I won't go! You can't send us out there, not to that creature!'

Out now in paperback from Red Fox at £3.50
1 THE SNOW-WALKER'S SON, ISBN 0 09 925192 2
2 THE EMPTY HAND, ISBN 0 09 925182 5
3 THE SOUL THIEVES, ISBN 0 09 953971 3